MA-L'S GRAND GATHERING

A report

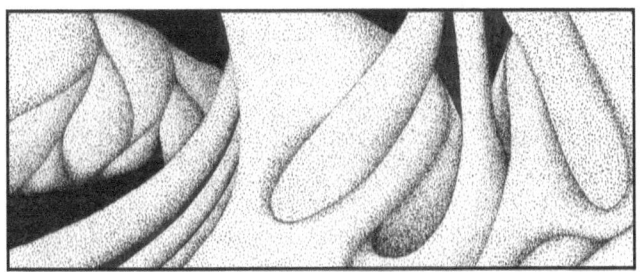

*An Improbable
Emergence
Book III*

Revised Edition

Ink works 1976 - 2017
Francis Voignier

Cover symbol: Warrior Ma-l's name

Library of Congress Cataloging-in-Publication Data
Voignier, Francis 1954 –   United States
Ma-l's Grand Gathering/Francis Voignier
ISBN-13: 978-1-7345551-2-7
ISBN-10: 1734555122

Fiction – Metaphysics – Arts – Philosophy

francisvoignier.com
Dolosse & Writs, Eureka, California

CONTENTS

PREFACE

As the unofficial story goes, one copy of *Ma-l's Grand Gathering* was left behind by an Angel on assignment in the Northern California region of Earth. The manuscript was brought to a medium who in turn, channeled a spiritual entity that went on transcribing its contents into a human-ready form. Nothing came of it – at least not until it was found in an attic and forwarded to me.

Another plausible version is that one of Marshall Slaughter and Geir Flemmingson's acquaintances from the Guild, brought the book over and left it behind, either intentionally or not. After all, three of the chroniclers, Angels Spencer, Vera, and Bluefeather have been frequently seen in both Reykjavík and at the Fieldbrook estate in Humboldt.

Whichever the provenance, the book is not technically part of the series that began with *The Disappearance of Olaf Swyndle,* and ended with *Convergence of the Realms* via *The Hektor Dilemma* – though it's undeniable that it fits squarely between volumes two and four. I leave it at yet another example of synchronistic manifestation – put simply, *Ma-l's Grand Gathering* was not intended to exist. One may say that a breach in the quantum field created by one of the many interpretations of the first two books by an unsuspecting reader, is responsible for it.

The most intriguing aspect of this whole affair is how this renegade book carries within it the seed of volume four which has not yet been written, but which is curiously already remembered as if from the past. Considering *Ma-l's Grand Gathering* will happen six hundred and forty-seven years outside a probable future of current Earth, it makes perfect sense.

The events depicted in the book happened after the severance of the Warriors' realms from the original Oneness, in celebration of the awakening of Ma-l, Xarn, and Enola's worlds, as well as the completion of the New Guild Center.

Seven chroniclers were chosen, not including agent Spencer who came in later. They were strategically positioned inside each domain and in various parts of the Great Hall, providing unprecedented perspective into the in and outs of the gathering. They and their fields go as follow:

- Angel Bluefeather – love
- Angel Monique – genetics
- Angel Gretchen – arts
- Angel Qo'ai-Marael – history
- Angel Khaldun – nuances
- Angel Grisha – intrigue
- Angel Vera – investigation
- Angel Spencer – security

I have read the manuscript numerous times with the aim of deciphering – beyond the central theme – the thread that links the reports to each other. I am convinced there is a lot more to the whole than the sum of its parts. I suppose it is not as crucial to know what exactly ties these elements together; as opposed to being cognizant there exists a concealed commonality between them.

I suspect the answer hides in Angel Bluefeather's question: "Why eight chroniclers when one would have sufficed?"

–The editor–

A CELEBRATION OF THE RISE OF THE REALMS

1 – INTRODUCTION

On day 1 of year 1 of the emergence of the realms, following the ceremony of the inauguration of Joonas Halls officiated by Great One Amaterasu, Goddess Ma-1 submitted the idea of a grand celebration to be enjoyed on her domain's grounds, in honor of all the key participants who played into making the emancipation of the Warriors' worlds a reality.

The festivities spanned a week's time and acted on many nuances, from subtle to remarkably exotic.

I was one of a team of chroniclers who paced the grounds during those unforgettable days and nights, with the task of documenting every aspect of the often complex interactions between the guests – each of us will take turns in the order that best befits the recollection of the event.

–Angel Bluefeather, Guild of Masters–

LIST OF GUESTS

Great One Amaterasu
Great Goddess Ma-l
Goddess Saka
Angel Olaf
Angel Vac
The Triad
Angel Leòn
Angel Ilia
Angel Axel
Marshall Slaughter
Geir Flemmingson
Snake
Angel Spencer
Angel Liv
Angel Naja
Angel Vera
Angel Lillian
Guild student Pau
Guild student Gerald Brinsk
Angel Shade
Angel Shido
Wolf the coywolf
Sam the dog
Angel Stefan
Angel Qo'ai-Marael
Great God Xarn and his tribe
Great Goddess Enola
Angel Lev

Also invited is the entire assembly of Masters and Guild students responsible for establishing the original Angel City and orchestrating the move into the New Hall.

Latest arrivals are welcome but access limitations will apply based on available space. No reservations.

Note: the G-day denomination stands for Gathering Day; it is tied to the Ma-lean calendar. G-day 1 represents the start of the celebration, while G-day -5 and G-day 3 respectively point to the fifth day before and the third one after it.

2 – EARLY RECORDS

Realms of Ma-l, Xarn and Enola
Place of activity: Great Goddess Ma-l's domain
Date: year 1 of the Ma-lean calendar, G-day -5
Chronicler: Angel Bluefeather
Department of Warrior and Realm History

Guests from Earth circa 2017 of *Probability Swyndle* – in commemoration of Angel Olaf's work – arrived early. Marshall Slaughter, Geir Flemmingson; Angels Liv, Spencer, Vera, and Lillian came in through the Keyhole Lake portal; and while the Masters attached to the Le Lien team went immediately to work at their sister headquarters in the New Guild Center (new name pending), the two humans joined Ma-l – the ex-Warrior and Great Goddess of her realm – to assist in the preparations. Vera and Lillian met with them shortly thereafter.

It was noticed upon arrival that a mutual affinity had developed between the human philosopher and Master Lillian – a fact most peculiar at the time since no Angel had ever gotten to that level of intimacy with an entity commonly referred to as "subject" for their quality of existing under the wing of protection and guidance. It was obvious the moniker did not apply to Earth denizen Geir Flemmingson. The nuance is recorded as the first-ever instance of mutually agreeable attraction between a physical being and a member of the Guild represented in the flesh.

The set-up was further enhanced by yet another unusual, if incomplete union – though they didn't know it yet: that of student Pau and Geir Flemmingson's friend Marshall Slaughter. Pau or Paula Hunter, a Guild defector who tormented the latter during the course of the extended case of the disappearance of Olaf Swyndle, worked under the supervision of Joonas, aka the Dove, founder of Hektor. I monitored a heightened level of coordinated affections between the two; thus, the rapport between the Guild student and the humanoid also stood as a curiosity – even more so since Pau was once a Hektor member, a group that despised all versions of humanity fitted with the original ego option.

But nothing compared to the deep union of Master Olaf and Great Goddess Ma-l. Not only had a relationship of sexual nature never been witnessed between an Angel and a deity – though I am not at liberty to disclose of another that existed under extremely different and necessary circumstances, while there were no means by which to witness and record it when it first happened, and to some extent, it has not yet manifested – but Master-to-be Olaf is of first-generation human stock which, by Guild standards, makes of the arrangement between the Goddess and the physical subject, astoundingly exotic – or in plainer terms – quite extraordinary.

And yet, I was once more taken by another convolution of the new Oneness, when it was revealed that ex-Warrior and Great God of his realm, Xarn, and humanoid and newly appointed Goddess Saka – spiritually born of Ma-l's dream from Great One Amaterasu's gift of light – had joined in a deep spiritual and sexual union, once again, involving the physical experience. In their case, the mix of developmental and evolutionary qualities is particularly unique, as well as deep-reaching.

Though my stylistic idiosyncrasies place some of the preliminaries of the main event in the past, this writing is undoubtedly vividly present, as I report from amid Goddess Ma-l's gathering of early, pre-festivity guests.

For now, it appears that after having worked in the kitchen for the last couple of days, professor Flemmingson and Angel Lillian have left to seek privacy; a wish that may seem futile amid such brouhaha, but Ma-l has arranged to have portals installed for signed-in users to access their allocated remote dwellings. The philosopher and Master Lillian's cozy nest is quite a ways downstream amidst an idyllic setting of copses and meadows. They are presently in the nude, swimming in a deep pool of turquoise water, splashing each other and laughing loudly. We shall respect their sacred space.

I have been looking for Master Vac, but he is nowhere to be seen. Angel Axel at Portals headquarters just informed me that he had business to attend, possibly with Great One Amaterasu. Vac remains as much a mystery as he is an inspiration to the Guild. Many have stipulated that he turned down the Ones' recommendation to join their ranks, in order to resume with an assignment he deemed of the highest importance – though, no-one in the Guild, or the domain of the Great Ones knows what that mission might be – at the exception, perhaps, of Amaterasu with whom he shares deep-reaching roots.

Angel Vera is replacing her friend Lillian in the kitchen. She is seen on and off taking turns between Goddess Ma-l and Master Olaf's stations, or joining the couple in the gardens for picking duty. Many students are partaking in the tumult, offering help from the catering capability of the Guild Center, but the hostess prefers to do it all from the bounty of her creation. There is great fire between the Goddess and her partner. I have permission to chronicle the consuming of that passion at its most intimate and vividly explicit, but I was told that the possibility of copies of the report being leaked, could lead to a misrepresentation of the sacredness of the celebration by some species, especially those still affected by the fear-based belief system of the de-spiritualized ego personality. So, in that light, I am still undecided as to whether I shall edit out some of the pseudo-offensive passages or not. I can safely say that their love-making is highly inspirational and beneficial to the new Oneness.

I should mention before I forget, that I have been assigned to the task of chronicling the subject of love, the quality at the base of all life and what sustains it. Others have opted for themes that best befit their unique personalities, such as the arts or the benign social drama of intrigue. Actually, Goddess Ma-l, who stands behind the creation of the history branch of the New Guild Center, recommended that I chose it as my subject. She said, "Bluefeather, you do 'love' like no-one else in this assembly; can I entrust you with accurately capturing its essence throughout the event?"

Certainly, she must have known that by nature, I would not have been able to stray too far from it.

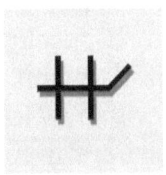

3 – A PRE-CEREMONY VISIT TO EX-WARRIOR AND GREAT GODDESS ENOLA'S REALM

Place: Great Goddess Enola's domain
Date: year 1 of the Enolaean calendar, G-day -4
Chronicler: Angel Gretchen
Department of Warrior and Realm History

Great Goddess Enola has opened her realm for anyone who wishes to visit it. Hers is 3rd to awaken after those of G-Goddess Ma-l and G-God Xarn.

Pending full synchronization, daytime varies between the three domains due to cycles that pulse to the personal beat of their respective creators. So, a Ma-lean day is somewhat longer than an Enolaean one, while a Xarnean period – though of the same length as a Ma-lean one – comes out slightly out of synch. Not bad in the light of a first attempt at merging timelines. Everything is relative, so even a reliable alignment will not change the fundamental makeup of their creations, including the inherent differences between their planetary and farther galactic arrangements. Portals will eventually take care of that.

While much is happening on the celebratory grounds over in GG-Ma-l's realm, there is quite a bit of action in the peculiar world of GG-Enola. It appears all the younger Masters are being drawn to her breathtaking city – she is the in-thing. Her reality is colorful – very colorful. It is essentially an art piece – a statement of one's miraculous gift of resilience done in bold visual strokes of exuberance. It is a playground born of the heart of a child; then framed by the hand of a master. Those familiar with the history of the Warriors will attest that there was nothing playful in the nature of their demise and predicament. GG-Enola's creation is an affirmation of the intrinsic joy at the very base of both Onenesses.

The Great Goddess' garb contrasts sharply with her environment, as if she wished to remain her own reminder of the past whence she came – both as a humble Warrior and a captive of the stone. Her clothing of choice, a one-piece, sleeveless, tan décolleté that ends at mid-thigh, hides very little of the extraordinary beauty of her youth and race.

She leads a horde of students and young Masters amid a maze of passages, tunnels, and overpasses that link all corners of her domain in near-limitless possibilities. Her sun is radiant in a way that highlights every single hue into a heightened state of luminescence. Though the colors are bright, they are far from glaring or harsh; there is an indescribable softness to them that betrays how carefully they were chosen.

GG-Enola is conferring with her entourage of Guild Masters and students on the options of populating her realm with mobile consciousnesses able to meld with the exoticism of their offered environment. Already, many species of flora and associated pollinators are lining the corridors of her city, branching out into new areas of grassy and sparsely wooded land, all the way past the walls of her central domain, into the semi-desert landscape of the land beyond. I hear many creative ideas being exchanged in playful outburst.

GG-Ma-l, G-God Xarn, and G-Saka join in at every possible chance, to the delight of the visitors from the New Center. Great One Amaterasu also came unannounced to give her blessings – Angel Vac was briefly seen by her side.

As Master in charge of reporting on everything artistic, I am particularly invested in probing the depths of the creator behind their work. Their background, upbringing, evolutionary marker and their commitment to the higher purpose of their unique incarnational or otherwise assignment, are grounds for remarkable and inexhaustible discoveries into the nature of the self and the greater gestalt of the Oneness. With every second – in physical terms – a new idea is born, a new skill – a re-invented version of the whole. GG-Enola's stark and alienating backdrop – the confinement to the stone that served as her psychological prison for the millennia that preceded the re-awakening of her vitality – represents what is essentially a black canvas. She proceeded from the absence of the vital resources needed by the creator. She had to conceive the tools, the medium, and the vision from the eye of a vortex in the early makeup of consciousness, invent purpose out of hopelessness, extract life out of near-nothingness, and find the necessary sustenance to keep the desire to live in the absence of love – an impossible condition by most standards. Yet here we are – her guests amid the splendor of that realized vision.

Masters come and go through newly installed portals that link Warrior Enola's world to the New Guild Center. Her reality is akin to a living museum of modern art, its walls in constant shape-shifting mode – its contents in a continuous state of metamorphosis.

It is beyond the scope of my assignment to extrapolate on the impact of such an extraordinary

10

achievement in the context of the whole. I recommend a closer look at what makes GG-Enola's world so special, and I hope I will be granted the privilege to assist in such an exploration on a long term basis.

For the present time, my work is to report on the nature of the relationship between the hostess and her visitors, in hopes of finding – with the other chroniclers – what it is that links the realms and the Great Hall to each other. So, in essence – even though it all started with the intention to focus on GG-Ma-l's grand gathering – the final product will most likely end up as a multifaceted study of this extremely important, symbolic moment. I am grateful to report from the sacredness of a place that sits very close to my heart.

4 – A LOOK INTO THE WORLD OF EX-WARRIOR XARN

Location: Great God Xarn's domain
Date: year 1 of Xarnean calendar, G-day -3
Chronicler: Angel Monique, genetics
Department of Warrior and Realm History

Wolf is the guide. He makes sure to inform me that I have a choice between using the portal to Great God Xarn's residence, or walking the long trail down the side of the canyon. Since I am a dedicated hiker and dressed accordingly, we descend the treacherous path, to the delight of the coywolf. He lets me know, with great pride, of his relations in the domain of Great Goddess Ma-l. I am endeared by his character, one from Xarn's palette of creations – hearing him heightens my sense of anticipation to meet the rightful steward of the land. There is a particular quality to the persona of the canid – he seems wholly comfortable with the knowledge of his origins, in a way that highlights his keen confidence in his own autonomy. He is an integrated spirit. He tells me there is no other like him in the realm; hence why he shares with me his affections for those of his kind in Ma-l's world. He is a fully adapted inter-realm traveler, and I gather – this should be dully noted – the first beyond the Warriors themselves.

We arrive within distance of the bridge spanning the river that separates our side from the cliff dwellings, where Xarn and his close tribe reside.

The Great God greets us. Like Ma-l, he is tattooed and naked. He stands formidable in his stature – the Warrior par excellence. Wolf takes the portal back to the top landing where he will await the next guest. Unlike Great Goddess Enola, whom I have only met briefly from a distance after the opening of her gate, Xarn is careful about who gets in, and as far as I know, I am one of the few Angels from the Center he has allowed into his world. He tells me Saka had a lot to do with it. Nonetheless, he is a charming host, humble and dignified. He asks why I wish to visit if the Guild's intentions are to chronicle the gathering in Ma-l's domain. My explanation of a setting that provides a backdrop to the event satisfies him. He compliments me on my looks and my fitness; also, he likes the way I speak – I thank him.

Xarn takes me to his dwelling in the cliff. It reminds me of the ones of Angel City, but with ample natural light entering from large openings instead of the artificial ambient glow of the Great Hall. He tells me Saka has just left to rejoin Ma-l in the kitchen. He speaks of her with love in his voice – Angel Bluefeather's department. Me, I am in genetics – loosely speaking, a specialist in all that is physical and evolves along a timeline. I am told Xarn's realm is unusual in its makeup for having only one specimen per species, yet each containing a combination of genetic codes. Though my field is irrelevant in the context of the gathering, I nonetheless hope it adds an element of exoticism to it, by highlighting variances not found in the original Oneness. I also count on exploring some of them further down the line.

I ask Xarn why he opted for singular representatives of his creations – he kindly explains:

"I have seen my original people couple up and build generation upon generation, only to witness humanity slowly descend into the bowels of madness. For now, my creations are eternal in their present form, unless they wish otherwise. No species can develop toward dominance. Of course, sex and reproduction are possible, but each offspring comes forward with a unique genetic code that takes on the characteristics of a new species."

There are a few hundred tribal members living amid the cliffs. Many more took to the wilderness of the lower canyon, to form the peaceful villages scattered along the river all the way to the sea. Representatives from each, visit at regular intervals to seek the proximity of their creator. Great God Xarn is well loved.

Upon hearing of the festivities, many seek to attend. They are rejoiced by the open invitations. A member of the farthest village approaches me; his name is Skatu. He is neither human nor beast, yet he is beautiful, while his demeanor is gentle and paused. He shows great affection towards his people, assuring me that each of them will eventually visit the Great Hall of the New Guild Center. I am delighted by the sheer authenticity that emanates from his being; it speaks volumes about the maker behind the spread of this enchanting universe.

Unlike the original Oneness whose physical sphere is represented by a single shared intergalactic expanse – though I must say, with infinite dimensional variations – each Warrior's realm is a complete universe, making the emerging Oneness an extremely complex and multifaceted gestalt that is best described as a multiverse. Xarn informs me of his dreams of inhabited orbs in his great sky and welcomes Angels to them. He says the collective spirit of their pioneers will be present at the celebration. I have an idea of the scope of what he is trying to get at, but I cannot in all sincerity, completely absorb the significance of his words. The concept of extraordinary genetic variations in the distant star systems of his realm overwhelms my senses. With permission, I could be here for a very long time indeed.

We go outside. He asks me to join him for a swim in the pristine waters of the river. I strip naked and indulge in the physicality of the moment – a rare treat. He says that I shall always be welcome in his world; hence, I can visit as I please – I am honored.

"No need for reservations," he adds.

I take it we are now friends.

5 – ACTIVITY IN THE GREAT HALL

Place of activity: The New Guild Center
Date: Year 1 of the Realms, G-day -3
Chronicler: Senior Master Qo'ai-Marael
Honorary Member, Department of
Warrior and Realm History

Since the early arrival of the Le Lien team members comprising of Angels Liv, Spencer, Stefan, Lillian, and Vera, the Great Hall has been aburst with movement. Not that the place was not alive before they joined – after all, there was the pivotal ceremony of the inauguration of Joonas Halls presided over by Great One Amaterasu – but the new volunteers from the Mother Guild made the bustle appear all the more official. Prior to it, there was of course the great move from Angel City to the New Center, which was fueled by much apprehension in connection with the missing codes for the access lanes to the Warriors' worlds. All is settled now, though most of the realms still need to open their doors.

While Goddess Ma-l is presently leading the march to the symbolic celebration that commemorates the true birth of the emergent Oneness, and consequently that of the New Hall, much is being shuffled around Angel affairs.

Team Qwave created the extraordinary system of communication that rides at zero-latency with nearly no artifacts, on the flux between Amaterasu and Saka's two stones. Hektor was neutralized without a battle, while our worst foe turned out to be our best ally under the dire last-minute circumstances that preceded great gestalt George's demise. The rise of Enola brought forth a flurry of activity amongst our young Masters and students. There is much to rejoice in the Guild's branch of the realms, on behalf of these remarkable news and accomplishments.

I was expressly asked by the elders to write about this episode in the budding history of the new Oneness, with special emphasis on the gathering in Ma-l's domain. Though most of us are born of the spiritual, we have chosen the physical experience to chronicle the event, mostly in appreciation of the key actors who made it all possible – notably, our human friends, Olaf, Marshall, Geir, and to some great extent, Saka, née Linda Sue. Although I am not known for my writing skills, the honor was bestowed upon me by my colleagues, in the light of my extensive work in the capacity of long-time chronicler of Guild history, to report from the vantage of my experience. My era takes us back all the way to the original team that foresaw the remote probability pointing to the emergence of a rare coalescence in a distant future, one that could only be reached by light under the guidance of Amaterasu, and to a wide degree, Master Vac, who is recognized by some of us as the original Angel – though that distinction has been known to belong to Amaterasu as well. But I shall not muddy the waters of the moment with tedious historical references – albeit it is my understanding that some of that history provides a suitable and lasting cushion for this precious and spacious present.

One of the main reasons for the great traffic, is the fact that volunteers have been flogging the Center in large numbers since Amaterasu opened the lane between the two

Onenesses. The path connects Keyhole Lake to Joonas Halls, the latter which acts as direct access to the hub of this still unnamed Great Hall – although a contest is in progress, while entries lean on the side of inventive humor.

At this very moment, it appears that turnstiles are relentlessly letting new arrivals in. Though I am fairly certain we have reached near-capacity and that no new Masters or students will be admitted until those ahead of them are dispatched into the realms.

The one beautiful thing about the new hall is that it has some element of natural light coming in – courtesy Snake, aka the great carver of stone, who refuses to tell where said light actually originates from. Of course, it's hardly more than a touch, but it reduces the cloistering feel of old Angel City. For the record, it is rumored the fire element chose its name in honor of Goddess Ma-l, who apparently is unfamiliar with the mythological dragons imagined by her root species.

As the result of the Joonas incident in the original Great Hall, students Pau and Gerald Brinsk, with guiding Masters Leòn, Shade, and Shido, have gathered around the idea of forming a support group for Angels returning from strenuous assignments, including the unfortunate ex-abductees of Hektor. Many such new groups have emerged around both novel and forgotten concepts, providing a much needed influx of new energy in the assembly; especially after these very long months of gestation in the old cavernous city. It is also evident the emergence of the new Oneness is having a beneficial effect on all, as the result of which, vitality abounds.

Much help is needed in many areas. Although my role is to report on what is currently happening, I sense I am on the cusp of being called to partake in some of the organizing around accommodating the new arrivals, especially since a contingent of elder Masters has made its choice of joining the Warriors' universes – needless to say, my department – and probably old acquaintances of mine. There is also the distinct possibility that the original team may be present in its entirety for the grand gathering – though I very much doubt any of them will stay beyond the celebration – but one never knows…

6 – EARLY RECORDS II

Zone of nuance: Great Goddess Ma-l's domain
Date: year 1 of the Ma-lean calendar, G-day -7
Chronicler: Angel Khaldun
Honorary member, Department of
Warrior and Realm History

––––––––––––

The guests from Earth -647 are arriving directly from Joonas Halls via portal. Probability Swyndle – or "OSw" for the techs in charge of collecting evolutionary data – is in direct line with the emergence of the Realms; thus, it is recognized as a past point of this present in physical terms – though it will not stay on that course for much longer. Those interested in the details may wish to check with the history department.

It is a first that two human subjects should be found amongst deities and Angels, but Professor Geir Flemmingson and investigator Marshall Slaughter are no ordinary humans. Without them, all of us doubt this day would have come to be.

Before I carry on, I volunteered to partake in the documenting of this gathering in my capacity of Master of nuances. Most are familiar with my work, but there are the few, especially among the techs, that seem discomforted by the ethereal nature of my specialized area. For the sake of simplification, I deal with the omnipresence of signals that may never be given a suitable environment for expression –

the tongues that piggy-back primary languages in the hope of reaching their obscure destinations – or which in most cases, end up looping in infinite redundancies. My main purpose is to usher these messages into the light. Of course, I am only reporting here – but work and play are elusive partners.

My intermittent involvement with the department has brought me up to date with the events that precede the emergence of the realms. It is why I know much about the misfortunes of student Pau as a pawn of Hektor under direct supervision of no other than Joonas the Dove, as well as her early relationship with the two humans. Through the play of nuances, this bit of history becomes rife with emotional, psychological, and spiritual twists and turns that tend to keep one such as myself, busy for eons. So, it is with particular interest that I observe the student's presence in the background of the early arrivals. According to Master Qo'ai-Marael, who heard it from Angel Leòn, Pau had been inquiring with Portals about the Earth contingent's estimated date of entry. When she got the news the humans and the Le Lien team had arrived, she immediately abandoned her duties at the recovery center and rushed to Joonas Halls, where she was informed that Marshall Slaughter and Geir Flemmingson had been forwarded to Goddess Ma-l's realm. She went after them with nary a hesitation.

In the light of Pau's past at Hektor, her actions pose a perplexing question: "What reason does she have to display such motivation?"

She has been cleared by Leòn and a panel of elders, and then reinstated as a student in the Masters' program. She has since demonstrated an extraordinary aptitude at showing deep compassion to those in pressing need of guidance and support – the Angel per excellentiam. So from the standpoint of my specialty, it calls for examining nuances in both her relationship with herself and the two humans. "Why not call it psychology?" one may ask. Well, the field of psychology is not among those of the Guild, as we all know.

Some will notice I am stating the obvious – the reason is that I was officially tipped that the report would be made available to specific sentient species, and that perhaps it was preferable to elucidate certain unfamiliar concepts – though I am unclear as to which qualifying species those may be.

So, there is Pau in the background. She looks uncomfortable and positively nervous; though I doubt her motives are anything but honorable. I cannot help notice that the nature of her scrutiny is aimed at the investigator, who is presently involved in a deep interaction with Goddess Saka on a subject of exquisite nuances. There is the love of friends between them, which I am sure Master Bluefeather will brilliantly elaborate on. That brief distraction is ample time to make me lose sight of Pau. Based on her auratic coordinates, she appears to have returned to the lower floor of the Great Hall.

Saka puts her index finger on Marshall's forehead. I hear her say, "The light never lies."

The nuances are healthy and indeed, there is light shining upon them.

7 – MEETINGS & ALLIANCES

Places of action: the Great Hall and Ma-l's realm
Date: year 1 of the Realms, G-day -2
Chronicler: Angel Grisha
Department of Warrior and Realm History

───────────

Finally, the last of the volunteers are being shown to their quarters. Many thanks must be given to the organizers – it was an exhaustive process. Upon reflection, Angels are not that much different from the humanoids they usher along the lines of their evolutionary travels. Consciousness is consciousness – it likes to stay busy. Since the physical element is the present environment of choice, it is difficult to tell who's who. I walk the Great Hall from corner to corner, visit each of the thirty-three floors that are accessed by the four stairwells; but because time is of the essence, I have set portals in various locations for efficiency's sake. Though in reality, meaning, beyond the material world, thoughts take me wherever I wish.

I believe we all have been instructed to write in a style that crosses over to various evolved societies and organized collectives of consciousness, but I'll let the translators deal with the details – most of us are common chroniclers, insomuch that style is not normally factored in.

Many of the Masters, who had been separated by lengthy and overlapping assignments, are reconnecting while enjoying rekindled friendships in the relative intimacy of the Center. All the tables and benches of the Great Hall and the two underground levels are taken with groups reminiscing about the olden days, or making cognitive adjustments. The most spoken subject is Hektor's forced migration into the simulated realms created by Great One extraordinaire, Amaterasu – I am a big fan of her work, but she unfortunately takes few students.

I feel like a spy, as I hear conversations I perhaps shouldn't eavesdrop on. It turns out that many Masters had originally agreed with the Dove. Consequently – because of his grand finale – these Angels now feel more at ease letting it all out about their thoughts of leaving the Guild at the time. A considerable amount of them chose faraway jobs as a means to distance themselves from their close allies, for fear they would digress too far from Guild protocol – others privately wished to create their own splinter groups. Now that it is all out in the open of the refreshing newness of change, amid the regrouping of once renounced alliances, words that had been kept silent are free to take their maiden flights onwards wherever such words find their field of fulfillment. Not in the realms, I hope.

There is no such issue with the Masters that came after the Ones entered in a contract with the Guild about facilitating the tribal uprisings that led to the wars against the so-called "Evil Spirits." The elders on the other hand, were a lot more divided than we thought – a first, I might say. I conclude with some uneasiness that there was a time when trouble was brewing in many corners of the League of Masters – many Angels in various shades of dark.

One could say that Hektor was once alive and well within the Guild; thence, I personally wonder how many more Tömörs roamed the corridors of its headquarters and traveled the many interdimensional lanes of its vast field of operation, trading information meant to remain confidential.

If Dahbar, Vexter, Tömör and their likes were allowed in this Great Hall, they would most likely be among these elder Masters, speaking with the same vehemence about how their opposition to the Great Ones and Guild guidelines, were all for the benefit of the release of the realms – all because of the Dove's last minute exploits. I hope that these words will eventually reach them so that they can recognize their own selves, and perchance, admit to the hypocrisy of the moment and come clean.

I am not at liberty to name the culprits – there are many – but I feel saddened as well as alarmed by their imposing presence in the New Guild Center, especially now that they seem emboldened by the relative protection of their pack reality.

I hope I am reading into something that is nothing more than a construct; that perhaps, my penchant for intrigue is making a mountain out of a molehill. I see Angel Qo'ai-Marael quite often as we cross paths in the Great Hall. She worked with Vac and Amaterasu in the pre-days of the Guild – her history credentials are unmatched in this Oneness. She is also the one that welcomed all the elders into the New Center. I am certain she can advise on how to ease my thoughts.

Speaking of Vac, he is seen roaming the floor in his usual manner, but he too appears rather perplexed. He is rarely seen alone in the Hall; most of the time, his presence coincides with Amaterasu's. Actually, he is coming my way as he seems to want to connect...

We walk away from the main floor to catch a portal to Joonas Halls. From there we enter into Ma-l's realm, and then through another portal to a place above a great valley.

"This is where I find the space to reflect, Grisha, a

gift from Ma-l – my own personal lookout," Vac tells me. "I take Wolf here with me on occasion – he has many companions on the plateau. But let me cut to the chase, my friend. You have – I am sure – been made aware of the many could-have-been Hektor members who wouldn't be here today if they had had the courage to join Joonas in helping him build his rogue league way back when. I welcome you to chronicle this short unscheduled meeting between us, well-knowing, mind you, that I have no jurisdiction in preventing you from doing so. Please keep me posted as you hear or suspect more. Amaterasu wishes me to stay on it and report to her. I am asking a great favor of you, Angel, but you have an official position in the Hall that practically makes you invisible. One thing though: do not speak to anyone about what you find besides me. As to the combined reports, they will not be published until all suspicions are allayed. Let's get to Joonas Halls; then we'll part from there."

It was brief – I am back in the Great Hall. Qo'ai-Marael waves at me from a short distance – what impeccable timing! I return the greeting but say nothing.

I am writing it all down – I can later decide what to keep and what not. My report is looking more like fiction and less like what I am accustomed to writing about at the department. I wonder if the other chroniclers are being faced with the same minor dilemma... "You are a master of intrigue, Grisha," the panel had humored; "go in there and pretend a coup is in the making!"

They laughed then, and hopefully, we can all laugh tomorrow.

8 – MA-L'S KITCHEN

Place of activity: Great Goddess Ma-l's domain
Date: year 1 of the Ma-lean calendar, G-day -5
Chronicler: Angel Bluefeather
Department of Warrior and Realm History

The kitchen is aburst with activity. Professor Geir Flemmingson and Angel Lillian have been replaced by Masters Liv and Vera, who are sharing their time between their work at Le Lien headquarters and picking vegetables in the garden.

Ma-l, Saka, Olaf, and the human detective are in charge of planning; they are presently directing volunteers from the student body to the various stations.

Earlier, the Great Goddess shared her thoughts with me about the possibility of closing the portals into her domain, on grounds that unrestrained amounts of visitors from the Center were distracting the workers, but she just confirmed that she had a change of heart. "It would present too many unnecessary complications," she admitted.

I made previous mention of the budding relationship between student Pau and investigator Marshall Slaughter; it is one of particular interest to me, since it's still vulnerable to probable outcomes that could rapidly change its course – though from my standpoint, it doesn't look like anything is threatening to interfere with the positively charged energy between these two.

I notice Angel Khaldun is very much taken by the student's awkward presence among the volunteers, for reasons which most assuredly veer off from mine. Let me simply say that Pau's sense of discomfort is called "being in love" – nothing more.

Yesterday, the student appeared immediately behind Marshall. She kept her distance mostly because he was speaking with Goddess Saka, who as it turns out, was the detective's aide under the name of Linda Sue Klein, on the case of Olaf's disappearance from his native world. The love between these two is the stuff of trusting friends; the kinds who opted out of sexual partnerships as the result of lessons wisely learnt from the traps of previous affairs – definitely a smart choice.

Whether Pau persuaded the members of her support group to volunteer for kitchen duty or not is debatable, but it does present the plausibility of a crafty maneuver on her part, one that solves the need for reasons of absence at the workplace. Angels Shade and Shido, as well as Master Leòn are on hand, busy with chores.

Angels Shade and Shido, now that's a match made in heaven – no pun intended! I very much like their energy, for it is the quintessence of the union of soulmates. No more solo assignments for Master Shido, and never one for lovely young Master Shade. For the record, and because of her cultural background, the latter's name could change like passing clouds, but she appears to be pleased with it for the time being.

Those are the players, but the real deal is what's being prepared under their deft hands. Love and food are notorious bedfellows, mes amis!

While wild grains and varieties of sweet acorn from previous gatherings are ground manually with heavy pestles in large stone mortars, some of the students are out harvesting new crops, drying fruit, smoking eggplants, and grilling peppers. Others, in the cold room, are making cheeses from the milk of large nuts donated by the villagers of Xarn's realm. Oils are pressed; wines are made from fermented berries; mead brewed from black locust flowers and honey. I hear that dried beans will be soaked tomorrow, ahead of being slow-cooked into stews and chilies. Fresh almonds and hazelnuts are crushed into pastes, mixed with spring water, poured into crock pots and covered until ready for their milk to be drained. Also, cured fish and poi will be provided, courtesy Xarn's tribe.

It is a long and complicated process generally handled by Guild technology through advanced ecological farming practices at our end, but it is fascinating to witness first-hand, the fine craft that went into preparing foods in the early phases of physical evolution. Some of our young Masters are very much invested in reviving these methods via the creation of small artisanal shops, traditional kitchens, and the practice of permaculture in collective settings, as part of the educational offerings to student recruits. I think it is simply brilliant.

Pau, who was outside in the gardens, finally enters the kitchen. She walks straight towards Marshall Slaughter, with only the slightest of hesitancy in her stride. My guess is that it's their first time reconnecting since she was rescued. Marshall had visited the realms once briefly with Geir and Amaterasu, but it is likely Pau was in Angel City at the time.

The investigator smiles at her as she extends her hand. He shakes it gently. They do not speak for long before Pau leaves; but not without slightly turning her body around and twice looking back at him before she exits. She seems genuinely shake – in a good of way. Marshall stands as he watches her leave before returning to his work. Saka observes the interaction – she appears rejoiced.

Angel Khaldun is also watching – he seems positively relieved. He smiles at me from the distance. He and I are very good friends.

Ma-l and Olaf are too leaving. They have their own secret portal and hideaway to which they gave me access for whenever I feel like escaping and chronicling from the vantage of their eagle's aerie – or so they humor.

I guess it is the hour at which all the lovers leave the kitchen, as I see Masters Shade and Shido catch a portal back to the Great Hall. I sense it is time for me to get acquainted with Angel Vera.

9 – THE ELDERS' ARRIVAL

Place of activity: The New Guild Center
Date: year 1 of the Realms, G-day -2
Chronicler: Senior Master Qo'ai-Marael,
Honorary member Department of
Warrior and Rcalm History

What a day it was reconnecting with old friends and orchestrating their dispatch to their accommodations – I had not seen some of them since the times of the Battles! Though many arrived as their original physical selves – at least, as I knew them back then – the majority came in the garb of their latest assignment. So the elder title, for those who are less familiar with Angel reality, is bound to contradict their looks, since they can appear quite youthful. We recognize the identity of a member, not by the clothes they wear, but by their unique signature, which in essence is akin to an indelible auratic code – one that, as we know, transcends the physical. It is why a Master like Angel Vac, is never mistaken for a common dog.

Three of these elders, (strictly referring to those who aspire to join the realms,) go all the way back to the pre-days of the Guild, when Great One Amaterasu, metaphorically speaking, lost her Angel wings to ascend to her present status. Two of them, Masters Jaco and Dzalarhons, traveled the eons with the original group, of which I was part with Vac and Joonas, to a time window that opened for a glimpse into this very part of history. Master Emile, also of the original team, opted to stay behind to take care of other affairs. Angels Theyia, Rashnu, Caax, Niamh, and Tealsky, among the many, were dominant players in making the Guild what it is today. I cannot stress enough the pleasure I have of knowing that the overwhelming majority of these elders – a group of nearly one hundred – are returning from far-apart assignments, to dedicate their time and skills to the realms. I am particularly honored by their presence here, for it can only point to a most auspicious scenario for the new Oneness. On the downside, the details of Hektor's exodus and the extraction of the codes by Joonas have to be explained, as the news did not always reach the confines of these Masters' work places. But I am glad to be of use in assisting them in finding where in the History Department, they can access that information. Based on the traffic on the site, I am to assume the subject awakens passions.

Masters Vac and Grisha are seen in each other's company, before quickly leaving the Hall. Portal spatial memory leaves no clue as to their destination – a private meeting most likely, though a bit strange at this time of reveling. Angel Grisha returns without Vac. He appears to want to address me, but refrains. I wave – he waves back.

Oddly, Master Dzalarhons stops by to inquire about Joonas's whereabouts, since records do not make any mention of them. History doesn't actually know besides what shows in the non-confidential part of Vac's report. Since the demise of gestalt George, it is established that he is to forever remain in the old réseau of caves and tunnels that were once meant to connect Angel City to the realms. Without the codes, they might as well be catacombs – a suiting final resting place. My answer amuses Dzalarhons.

"I shall ask Vac in person," she says.

I find it mildly vexing that my words do not seem to satisfy her, but for anyone who knows the Master, her attitude is on par with her character – logical and insatiable.

Down on the first underground floor, where the gates to the arrested realities reside, and where one may wish to access Snake's underworld, student Pau and Masters Shade, Shido, and Leòn return from one of their shifts at Ma-l's gardens and kitchen. While I sense Leòn knows the true meaning of their volunteering in the preparations, the young Angels are oblivious to it and for good reason – love is a beautiful thing. It is just an intuition on my part, for I do not see the aim, and Pau is not allowing me to read her, but I believe she is concealing her true motives. I assume it is all inclusive of a silent understanding between them: the student does her student thing, as the Master observes with keen endearment. Or perhaps, I am just reading into something that is not what it seems – the more you know, the less you know...

At any rate, now that the elders have all settled in, I can resume, unimpeded, with my work for the Department of Warrior and Realm History; though it may be an overreaching bit of wishful thinking, since these old acquaintances are eager to converse and get updated on the current state of affairs around the New Center. I had expected their desire to help the realms would have come with substantially more preparation and research, so I am somewhat surprised by the oversight. It is possible these Masters seek a front view into the emerging Oneness as a symbolic reward for their seniority – not very Angel-like of them, if I may say so. But again, it is not my best quality to assume without cause. As a matter of fact, I find it odd that I should doubt their integrity; it definitely isn't a typical

Angel thing to do either. Anyway, my scattered thoughts are probably outside the scope of this report...

The Hall is now at full capacity. Many Masters are in Goddess Enola's magical world, being tourists – nothing more exotic than a completely new realm of consciousness unexplored by the Guild. No wonder Hektor wanted in so badly. Many are also visiting Ma-l's domain and getting enamored by her gardens and the beautiful trails along her valley. Anyone looking for serenity should definitely pay her land a visit.

I am now standing on the balcony of floor thirty-three, stairwell three, overlooking the Great Hall. Master Jaco surprises me as he emerges from the tunnel that leads to Goddess Ma-l's realm, which in spite of Snake's new work, is still blocked at its end. I tell him we use Joonas Halls to access her domain.

"Yes, indeed, I came to a rather insurmountable obstruction," he says.

The New Center denizens greatly favor the doors of Amaterasu's design over the antiquated tunnels – though without these latter passageways holding the codes, the grey doors of the Halls would be inoperative.

I explain to Master Jaco how the collapse of the mother reality ended up doing much damage to the realms, consequently shutting down some of the original lanes. I offer him the use of my temporary work portal to reach Ma-l's place, but he declines. He wishes me a good day then goes for the deep stairwell.

I suppress my thoughts from asking that one pertinent question – instead, I simply say goodbye.

Back on the Hall floor, I meet with Master Emile, who is having a grand time interacting with both residents and visitors. He hugs me, telling me how wonderful things are in the New Oneness. He is just returning from Goddess Enola's city – he is absolutely delighted. He brings warmth to my heart. Out of curiosity, and perhaps for the sake of perspective, I ask what made him wish to join the realms.

"Over the months that preceded my decision, I spoke with all those at Le Lien, Qwave, and elsewhere who were involved with the Swyndle case from its inception; namely Vac and Amaterasu. With the full kindness of agent Liv, I got the in and outs on the program that took Joonas to the simulation of Guild Headquarters. I became extremely familiar with all the players, including Jarred Gulliver who is not among us for reasons well explained by Angel Lillian. It's a very long road, but I became enamored by their story – I couldn't wait to be part of it," he answers.

"Very sobering to hear you say it as it is, dear friend," I return.

I feel much better – the day is still young.

10 – FOR VIGILANCE'S SAKE

Places of action: the Hall and the realms
Date: year 1 of the Realms, G-day -1
Chronicler: Angel Vera, team Le Lien,
Guild archivist

I've now been on both sides of this case – though technically it's no longer one.

I know everything there is to know about the realms and the participants that made it all happen. Le Lien is the branch that deals with trouble when trouble occurs – which doesn't mean we create it – or wish for it to happen. When it's not around, we do the other things we like to do. I enjoy snooping around and taking notes, so I asked the history department if they could use another hand with a pen. I also volunteer in the kitchen with my best girlfriend Lillian, her beau Geir, and his good friend Marshall who's also my good friend. I believe Lillian and I, with Liv and Spencer, in tandem with The Triad, were the first Angels to fully enter in an open contract with humans and work as a team. I'm proud of it – especially considering it brought us all here together at the eve of a celebration for the ages.

A few days ago, I met Angel Bluefeather and we hit it off. I needed a healthy dose of love – no strings attached.

To Earth's folks who will read these words: know that there are fundamental differences between your Angels and us – but I digress.

So, because we don't expect trouble, I'm not looking for it. That being said, vigilance is still de rigueur, as what we have here appears to be a large contingent of Angels that have not been seen together since trouble was the Guild's middle name – just a reflex on my part.

Anyway, I'm just supposed to be chronicling from the vertex of my volunteer duties – namely the kitchen, whence I survey the gardens and the cabana. I interact with curious visitors, lost students, working crews, etcetera. But hey, I'm not blind – if I see something outside the usual, I'm not going to pretend it's not there.

So, here comes Master Caax, founding elder, and an old acquaintance of the Dove, who looks like he's nonchalantly sniffing around. He's one of the many that hasn't been seen at headquarters for centuries in Earth's time. Then, Angel Niamh materializes right in his tracks. Again, she is one on a long list of absentees who's been stationed out of the way since the Great Battles. Furthermore – and for the sake of making a point – I stumble across Master Tealsky, an old friend of Niamh, who's walking the paths of Ma-l's gardens, looking distracted and positively out of place – she too has not been seen around the Guild for eons. The same goes for another hundred or so of them.

So, no, I'm not on the job – but it feels like the job is on me!

Usually, my work involves dealing with exo-cases, stuff outside the league. But the treachery of Tömör has left a bad smell outside the skeleton closet of the elders who got their panties in a bundle around the decision by the Ones to rescue humanity and contract the Guild for the job. As investigator Slaughter would say, "I smell a rat even though it's the last critter on my list." – Tacky, but to the point.

So, yes, I smell a rat. I tell Spencer and Liv, who ask me to please keep a lid on it – which in Le Lien terminology means the use of utmost discretion. In other words, I go on doing what I'm doing, while staying vigilant – no need for overreaching, even in the light of the recent Hektor fiasco.

Lillian and Geir return from their daily escapade – it's about time. I have been feeling ambushed by my own observations, so I could use the comfort of a few friends around. Saka comes in with Xarn with more supplies from his realm. Laughter is back in the kitchen and it's a very good thing – I love to laugh.

Today is a big day, with the Grand Gathering on track to start tomorrow. Most of the official guests are now on location, and those who haven't already been present through their work, are being oriented to their assigned quarters.

Lots of cooking is going on – big pots everywhere, volunteers kneading dough, loaves being pulled with long peels out of the earth ovens, pies cooling off on wood racks – the works. Volunteers are setting tables outside in the meadows, building stages for musicians, poets, and comedians. Enola is in charge of décor with "her people." That girl knows how to grow a crowd – half the Guild's students are magnetized to her. It's going to take a special team to pull them out of their collective trance. But I must admit that I'm endeared by it.

Great Goddess Ma-l has been extremely busy, to say the least. Today for the first time, she didn't enjoy the opportunity to run off with Olaf and take care of personal matters, whatever they may be.

Xarn returns to his realm – he never likes to stick around much – but Saka stays behind to help the hosts.

Surprise, surprise – here come Amaterasu and Angel Vac with a furry companion! I know of the visitor from the case files – his name is Sam; he belongs to Saka's old friend Maggie Phillips, back on Earth -647, *Probability OSw*. Sam is known for tricks that have somewhat confounded fundamental interdimensional laws – personally, I attribute those qualities to his blissful state of being. He's not sure where he is and why, but he seems OK with it. Saka runs to him and hugs him with boundless joy in her heart – got to love the girl!

Sam walks to the creek's waterfall and hangs out there for a while.

Vac goes over matters with Amaterasu.

If I am not mistaken, all the important players are now among us, at the exception of Joonas and his once-guise, Jarred Gulliver, both excused due to particular circumstances.

Vera out.

11 – THE STAY IN XARN'S REALM

Location: Great God Xarn's domain
Date: year 1 of Xarnean calendar, G-day -2
Chronicler: Angel Monique, genetics
Department of Warrior and Realm History

———————

While much is going on in Great Goddess Ma-l's realm and in the Great Hall, I decide to spend more time with my host and his tribe. It's a behind-the-scene view which I deem just as important as what is going on in the foreground. It is like being close to the roots of the action, or the deeper mechanics behind the realization of all events.

Many villagers travel with their goods, some all the way from the sea with cured salt fish and a genus of coconut I am unfamiliar with – I make note of it. Even though *la physionomie* of these individuals differs greatly from one another, I can now discern the string that connects them all: it's in their mannerism, their gentleness, the way they smile and engage – it's in the warmth of their hearts. They are curious but not invasively so. We communicate telepathically though they do speak a multilayered language that parallels their genetic makeup. They are massively intuitive with acute cognitive abilities and unique skills of adaptation. Their presence puts Xarn's creational adroitness at a very high mark. I wonder if the new Oneness is not the conglomerate of multiple universes, each on the level of our native One – the thought is staggering in scope.

The methods of reproduction among these residents are of two related variances: via sexual intercourse when the physical makeup allows for it; or the internal mechanics of dual gender attributes of different genetic builds. In all cases, the offspring are born with at least two distinct species strains – something quite remarkable in my line of work. Great God Xarn's work wanders across assumed impassable gaps, onward to where known genetics meet with their mathematical counterparts in marriages not found in the makeup of our All That Is.

Once again, how does all of this relate to the main topic of celebrating the realms? I believe it does in all of its splendor by exposing diversity never encountered before. To a great extent, it parallels the connections made between different levels of consciousness as seen by the various alliances between humans, Angels, and deities, on the grand platform of this gathering.

Wolf reports an incident of breach. Xarn appears mildly concerned. I ask permission to eavesdrop but he advises that I stay out of it. In fact, the two walk away for privacy. A breach by whom, I wonder?

Xarn comes back and apologizes for the unmannerliness. "Someone who must have gotten lost in the portal system," he says.

I know little about the depths of portal works but I sense there is more to it.

Two of the villagers – I call them Jessie and Alice – a male and female of compatible physicality, desire to visit the realm of the Great Goddess Ma-l. They carry their supplies of dried nuts, fruit, and varieties of leaf-wrapped root pastes in wicker baskets hanging from milkmaid's yokes. The weight does not concern them – their loads could very well be floating from my perspective. Xarn approves of their request, so I offer to show the way to the Goddess' land.

Xarn and his close tribe bid their farewells. Alice and Jessie refuse to take the portal to the top of the canyon. They walk ahead with their fares – I follow with Wolf behind. The canid is by far more talkative than his maker. I don't ask – he just volunteers the information. The intruder was a Guild Master, as per the colorful description forwarded by the coywolf. Xarn has not authorized access into his realm, which means the codes were tampered with. Wolf doesn't know that, but it's an easy guess from an Angel's standpoint. I will report to Vera at Le Lien about it and leave it at that. We don't have a name, while Wolf's description leans in the direction of the fantastic, so nothing may come of it. "Twas a female," he says though.

Alice and Jessie make it to the top with no apparent effort – these people are super-specimens who work in tandem with their environment – as in being one with it. Crossing over into Ma-l's realm doesn't change a thing – they adapt seamlessly. I am overtaken with wonderment about *le merveilleux monde de Xarn*. I feel reassuringly warm in my soul.

12 – NUANCES BEYOND THE KITCHEN

Zone of nuance: Great Goddess Ma-l's domain
Date: year 1 of the Ma-lean calendar, G-day -5
Chronicler: Angel Khaldun
Honorary member, Department of
Warrior and Realm History

I was worried for student Pau, but my fears now stand unfounded. She is in love with investigator Slaughter, yet her kind of love is tied to pain from the past, to remorse as in a nuance of guilt. She is caught between two selves: one she has left behind, but from which she still bears the weight of suspicion, as if it were to return unannounced; the other – actually her core self – which she is afraid may slip through the meshwork of an unforgiving fate. She is a minor character in a Greek tragedy; she does not die a dramatic death while the world collapses around her last words at the fall of the curtain; no, she sits in a forgotten corner of the stage, in the shadow of honor, resigned to live a life of misery, forever unappreciated... It is of course overreaching on my part, for there are no dark corners in the settings of this stage – what is being played rather, is on the side of cheerfulness. But as far as nuances go, I hope the reader gets the drift.

Marshall Slaughter leaves from his post in the kitchen; his shift is over. He goes outside as Pau, who, based on her auratic signature, is arriving from the Great

Hall, walks towards him briskly. The two follow the creek downstream. I get permission from both to read the nuances of their conversation. Pau braves the moment and goes for it – her proposition is well received. It is clear Marshall very much cares for his ex-tormentor – there is great understanding and compassion in his heart. I have enough of the details to know all is going well between them; thus, I am extremely delighted for the student – she has made a remarkable recovery from the trauma of Hektor. I do no longer need to concern myself with her affairs; the page is turned. Goddess Saka is observing their return from a distance with great interest. I think I now understand what she meant when she said the light never lied. Friends would know that about each other.

Angel Bluefeather is in an active discussion with Angel Vera. There are no nuances there; it's all in the open. They laugh, knowing there can only be good things ahead; and being acquainted to the both of them, it's easy to guess what that might be. There is a quality in the air of Ma-l's realm that has a unique effect on sex drive, which makes me wonder about the other realms and their attributes...

There are more nuances, or rather, counter-nuances that have caught my attention. Some of the visitors, whom I have seen gathered around tables in the Great Hall, now act like strangers to each other, as they stroll through Ma-l's gardens. I have been around the Guild for a long time; I swear I have never been exposed to their signatures or heard their names being spoken. Angel Bluefeather informs me they are elders back from distant assignments.

Still, they are unreadable. Most Masters consider the practice of guarding the self, antiquated and pedantic. Why hide when you can be free? That is pretty much the norm of the glorious present, but not all agree.

"Take Angel Vac for instance," Bluefeather tested, "do you read him?"

I have to admit that Vac is hard to guess, but I have trust that if I ask, he is going to tell. On the other hand, the outside nuance in regard to these elders does not inspire the need to know. I deem it a fundamental distinction.

Angel Bluefeather sees where I am coming from.

"I cannot feel the love in their souls," he confesses. "Perhaps they suffer from post traumatic stress – kindness may help."

He's right – I get his point.

Ma-1 and Olaf left a while back; only Masters Vera and Liv remain to instruct the volunteers. Angel Bluefeather offers to partake in the chores, so I feel like joining as well. It turns out to be a very sound choice. The mind gets released when the body takes over. There is much to do, we get sweaty then we go to the creek to cool off and return to work some more. Angel Liv is vibrant but seems absorbed. She and Spencer are known to be married to their work. I respect the sanctity of her space.

I realize that beyond good company, the kitchen is also the ideal place from which to observe.

13 – MEETINGS & ALLIANCES II

Places of action: the Great Hall and Ma-l's realm
Date: year 1 of the Realms, G-day -1
Chronicler: Angel Grisha
Department of Warrior and Realm History

After yesterday's meeting with Angel Vac, I have been thinking. I am a historian with a fondness for the dramas of a civilization's rise and fall, so I have a tendency to anticipate the spikes and dips of ages. It was my job at the history department of the main Guild and I plan on making it mine as well in the realms. What I recorded then, happened inside the universes we surveyed – not within the society of Angels. I am not a reporter of internal affairs; that is the area of Le Lien. In other words and with all due respect, I feel at odds with Master Vac's request to eavesdrop on the elders' conversations, or profile them based on behavior. The aura of court intrigue around the favor that is being asked of me is to be entertained by those with colorful imaginations; but then again, that would be in the context of playacting – which this is not.

That being said, and regardless of Vac's input, I am the one, who in my own words, set the intrigue in motion yesterday; hence, I have to take responsibility for it. To get to the point, I started to doubt myself. I woke up with remorse for having had a conspiratorial sentiment towards these senior Masters. There is an internal conflict at play, fed by the paradox of the uneasy marriage of trust and suspicion; trust being at the base of all things-Angel, while suspicion is imported from unused potential, often triggered by external dynamic agents. I am not one known for my impulsive behavior, so this surprises me.

Part of me doesn't want to be remembered as the Angel who erred on the side of fantasy, but frankly, that is somewhat vain. I shall continue chronicling the event, and if something jumps at me, only then will I go on to honor Vac's request.

I am greeted by Angels Qo'ai-Marael and Emile on my way to one of the Hall cafeterias. My female colleague introduces the elder Master; I find him charismatic and extremely engaging. The day is on a good start.

At the cafeteria, more founding Angels are seen assembled in groups, while students and younger Masters go in and out, opting for the vast open floor of the Great Hall instead.

An elder at one of the tables appears to seek my attention – I walk to the group. She introduces herself as Master Theyia. I nod in the direction of her three companions who greet me in return – they are Jaco, Rashnu, and Lo-shen. Master Jaco belongs to the first team that included Vac and Qo'ai-Marael, while the other three are founders of the Guild.

"We see you walk the Great Hall, entering notes on your handset," Theyia said. "We hear that the grand gathering is not only to be chronicled for historical purpose, but for the publication of a précis for the pleasure of Angels and members of sentient species as well, am I correct?"

I am about to answer with a detached affirmative, but then, I need to clarify.

"The idea of a précis was never tossed my way, but I am sure a comprehensive version will be available through the department."

Theyia ignores my response.

Master Jaco comes forward.

"We understand the event is being followed with great interest, and much begs for documentation, but isn't it a bit of an extravaganza to make of a mundane celebration a historical landmark – whose idea is it?"

I explain that the historical significance is not in the celebration as much as it is in the reason for the gathering, and that Ma-l's party is strictly symbolic.

"A great time for the Guild," I hear from Master Lo-shen on my right.

"Allow me to elucidate," I offer, "It is only a Guild achievement it the way it epitomizes the adaptive skills of Angels in the face of diminishing possibilities. It is as much the collective work of our human friends and the three realm Warriors, as it is the one of Amaterasu and the Guild."

"Are you saying that without the humans, the emergence of the new Oneness was not foreseeable?" Jaco added.

"That is correct," I reply with mounting discomfort.

"It is an interesting theory, but the laws of probability certainly entertain greater variations than a mere singularity," he lets out.

I do not wish to counter the Master; he is forceful and intimidating. His might is indisputable, but it raises flags which I would prefer had remained unfurled.

"You may wish to speak with Great Goddess Amaterasu, who, I believe, is presently part of Ma-l's guests. Historians such as myself prefer to stay on the side of verifiable facts. Humans did indeed play an undeniably instrumental part in the rise of the new Oneness. Whether their presence defines an absolute in the realization of this historical moment or not, I am not at liberty to opiniate."

I then explain that I have work to do and look forward to meeting again. They understandably smile.

"Until next time," Master Rashnu says with a low hand wave.

I pick up a Russian Caravan to go – a quirky morning ritual in memory of my last assignment – and walk back the way I came, past Qo'ai-Marael and Emile still deep in words.

I sit on a bench next to a student, reflecting on what just happened. It's not an issue of me imagining anymore; Master Jaco used calculated provocation to carry a subliminal warning that presages a current aimed at imposing a different kind of order into accepted thinking. I have never felt that sort of energy coming from an Angel before. I am now back to where it all began, except this time, I no longer doubt myself.

14 – FOR VIGILANCE'S SAKE II

Places of action: the Hall and the realms
Date: year 1 of the Realms, G-day -1
Chronicler: Angel Vera, team Le Lien,
Guild archivist

———————

Back from my half-shift at Le Lien.

I'm not at liberty to tell, but what I can say is that something's up with some of the elder Masters – it's now official. There have been reports from various Angels who have been put through the trust test in their presence. Too much of a coincidence for a conspiracy, yet it's still too early for a verdict.

I've been asked to get back to the kitchen in my capacity of security agent, but the team insists that I keep on chronicling as part of the "open policy."

Even though the kick-off is set for tomorrow, the party might as well be on – all the rock stars are onstage – except for us, meaning me, Liv, Spencer, and apparently Vac, who are acting the role of the ever-watchful audience. I have been briefed on whom to keep an eye on – Dzalarhons tops the list. The other major suspects are Jaco, Caax, Theyia, Tealsky, Rashnu, and Niamh, followed by another fifty-or-so minor players.

Why are they suspect? As I have previously mentioned, they all are elders who showed up synchronically out of the nowhere of their extremely remote assignments – the same way they left at the time of the rise of Hektor. The first particular is the reality they didn't come here out of conviction – in fact they know little of the events that helped propel the realms. The second is that they all knew Joonas personally, though all opted out of Hektor. One may say that choice is enough to exonerate them, but Le Lien thinks otherwise – I agree.

I'm not permitted to tell any more about the meeting, but if I see something, it's all up for grabs.

Bluefeather and I were down for some prime time – instead I'm back on kitchen duty – it sucks.

Lookee, Jaco is making a grand entrance! He assesses the scene. Now, he sees Amaterasu and Angel Vac – he walks straight to them. I seek permission to tune in from a distance – to my surprise both the Great One and Vac grant it. Besides small talk about "the olden days," I don't get the impression of closeness. Amaterasu expects Jaco to get to the point – it arrives in the form of a vague allusion to how well the humans performed against expectation – how subtle. Vac reminds him of his involvement in the original travels to the pertinent probability. "How could I forget?!" the elder sputters. He mentions his earlier talk with Qo'ai-Marael – he wants to know more. Amaterasu hits him straight on:

"For someone who seeks to work for the realms, it is clear you skipped on the material that would give you reason to want to do so; unless your reasons have nothing to do with the achievement we are in the process of honoring."

Jaco feigns indifference.

"I have always favored extreme assignments in the farthest of locations – my choice couldn't be more simple or logical," he flexes.

51

"Indeed," Amaterasu returned.

She wishes him a good time at the festivities then walks away. I feel privately rewarded by the Great One's move – she has what she needs. Vac stays with Jaco but permission to eavesdrop has expired. I connect with Liv who's on active duty – she's on Jaco, but informs me of Niamh and Caax's recent entrances. I sense the place is about to teem with troublemakers.

So yes, why are these guys being targeted? Simple: they trigger stuff in younger Masters that has never been recorded. We get these reports of confused Angels, who feel viscerally drawn to intuitions that weave against the fiber of Guild protocol, namely doubt and mistrust. Anything shady that is not expected is suspect – elemental.

Yet another thing that personally affects me is the fact these Masters are not on the list of pre-celebration guests. Sure, it's open to anyone, but etiquette dictates good judgment – sorry!

As I've said on occasion, we're not perfect – I have my moods. Bluefeather and I were on for some well-deserved, sublime release – instead I have to wash dishes and keep an eye on elder so and so.

Liv always says of Lillian and me that we behave like humans; I guess we have taken on so many Earth assignments that they have rubbed on us – nothing to be ashamed of. Talking of Lillian, she's also out there working her butt off instead of shagging Geir – no rest for the wicked! Actually, the philosopher is conversing with Marshall, Saka, Olaf, and Bluefeather – I have no doubt based on demeanor, as to the topic being discussed.

Master Lo-shen catches me by surprise:

"What gives you the privilege to skip on all the fun, Angel," I hear her ask from behind.

She smiles – it's a good smile.

"Some girls just know how to do it right," I respond candidly.

"Indeed – my name is Lo-shen," she says

"Your name precedes you, elder founder."

"That information betrays your trade, Vera."

"I had no intention to keep it to myself," I counter.

The gorgeous Asian Master fascinates me – I'm almost certain she's clean. She reminds me of members of the pre-Le Lien agency that served the Guild under the difficult days of the Great Battles.

"*Third Eye*, I presume," I hear myself say.

She smiles once more.

"I am sure you and I will talk again soon – good luck with the chronicling," she returns.

She leaves with a touch to my shoulder, as if to hint at a silent understanding.

I'm not sure where she's at, but I would date the girl in a heartbeat. Oh, my poor mind!

Bluefeather must have sensed something. He comes to me – arms outstretched – and gives me a melter of a hug.

"Take me away from here," I beg.

15 – SEX & AFFECTIONS

Place of activity: Great Goddess Ma-l's domain
Date: year 1 of the Ma-lean calendar, G-day -1
Chronicler: Angel Bluefeather
Department of Warrior and Realm History

———————

It's indisputable that without love there's no life; therefore, it goes without saying that love should be the main theme at the birth of an unimaginable Oneness – its presence can be felt all around. Take the villagers from Xarn's realm for example: I've never come across such gentle and loving individuals in any species out of the thousands I have interacted with. Also, the unions across the various levels of consciousness, as well as the boost in multilateral growth – so unique to these very realms – overwhelm me with joy.

The symbolic moment was when Ma-l and Xarn made love for the first time. It was the crossing at which all the elements of their worlds coalesced. The Great Goddess was kind enough to share her memories with me. She remained a virgin as a Warrior; sex was enforcedly forbidden. Through repression, its drive served the forces of rage and aggression. Later, as a lone budding Goddess, she made love to her land, becoming one with it. When she began desiring physical contact with Olaf, she feared the divide between them was too wide to span. With Xarn inside her, it was as if she had been set ablaze, while the cool waters of his being flowed in between the fingers of her fire, intertwined but never touching. It was the marriage of two realms; thus, in that moment, an alliance was created that could never be severed. Goddess Enola is wedded to her art, but she too will experience that love when the air of her reality mixes with that of Ma-l and Xarn's realms – or when another door opens in Joonas Halls.

At any rate, I eventually accepted the invitation to visit Ma-l and Olaf's love nest – it was an education in a field in which I thought I was the expert. Angels do not need words to feel what I felt; it's all interweaved in the syntax. Our friends from other lands and cultures will have to simply let their imaginations carry them to the private places of their desires. The sacred sexual act cannot be dragged down the dark psychological alleys of Earth and other quasi-hospitable planets; therefore I refrain from the descriptive. They are both gorgeous beings, their love-making is sublime – worlds are born of it – that is all that needs to be said. Their union is the perfect example of the boost in consciousness I speak of – Olaf went from the somewhat evolved human stage, to being invited as a young Master; to now finding himself on the cusp of becoming a God of the realms.

Anyway, the pre-party is on and everyone's here. Lovely Vera is stuck behind the kitchen counter, giving me the smile of someone whose fun has been robbed, but she takes it philosophically. Actually, in the process, mine has been undermined as well – but we tell each other it's OK with a telepathic nod.

I am noticing elders who aren't on tonight's list, and frankly, I don't think they belong here – their hearts are like coals, or voids for that matter. They're akin to the casino coolers that turn lucks around. What's up with these Angels? One is particularly dark; his name's Jaco, I've been told. He connects with Amaterasu and Vac, but soon the Great Goddess leaves to join Saka and Xarn who are engaging with some of the villagers and Angel Monique. Just then, Saka excuses herself to connect with Marshall, Geir, and Olaf – I have found my group!

The humans from Earth are particular in two ways: first, they have a hold on philosophy – second, their love-making does not hinge on the biological drive to perpetuate their race. We let them keep the philosophy since it's part of their evolutionary makeup, but we stole the sex – and then improved upon it. Three of the four here know that, since they have experienced the elevated versions of Angel and deity foreplay, intercourse, and climax. Marshall should soon find out what a student of the Guild is capable of. I hear Pau is returning to Earth -647 with him to finish her studies. Only good things can come of it.

The fulcrum edge of humanity's development has always been narrowly tied to its median point in favor of a slight positive, which has allowed for a slow evolution. The presence here of Geir and Marshall, and in the light of Olaf and Saka's rapid metamorphoses from their previous selves, is a strong indicator of that point's significant shift. I hear Olaf's work is sending ripples into spheres far beyond his world – quite remarkable for his native species. The human race, in the philosopher and the investigator's version of reality, is at the center of the delicious paradox of being on course with the emergence of the realms, while simultaneously veering off the one of the collapsed mother reality. I sense my work in their world is about to become exponentially more pleasurable, if perhaps somewhat less academic...

16 – THE FIRST MORNING

Place: Great Goddess Ma-l's domain
Date: year 1 of the Ma-lean calendar, G-day 1
Chronicler: Angel Gretchen
Department of Warrior and Realm History

GG-Enola and Angel Lev are busy putting final touches to the décor. Performers from G-God Xarn's villages and the Guild's student body are readying themselves while going over schedules. I am mesmerized by the multi-species individuals from the God's realm – their hearts are just as musical as they are gentle. They never rehearse – each of their sets is an evolution of the previous one. The younger students favor the louder and more progressive performance style of some of Earth's dance and theater institutes, while music tends to lean towards grunge. Equipment and power – when necessary – are provided by Qwave. GG-Ma-l favors the less cacophonic forms of artistic expression though, so she has the loudest stage positioned at the farthest end of the main grounds.

It is said the Goddess contracted Snake for the bonfires that will burn throughout the gathering; that in of itself is testament to the might of her realm, as well as the powers she summons.

Last night's pre-ceremony was mostly for friends of GG-Ma-l's, essentially the main characters in the grand play of the emerging Oneness. So, I found it peculiar that a number of elders showed up as if they were in the process of evaluating real estate – it was rather discomforting from the standpoint of the artistic mind. I wonder how many of the guests were affected by their presence.

I point my observation to Angel Lillian who's among the early risers. She says she can't tell much, but is aware other Chroniclers share my unease. She advises that I spend time with Masters Emile and Lo-shen to counteract the profiling effect. "They too are founders, but you will find them most accommodating," she adds.

I sense Lillian knows more than she is willing to tell, but I refrain from asking – I prefer to stay close to my heart and the work of GG-Enola.

Not enough is being said about what went into the layout of the grounds. GG-Ma-l gave her Warrior kin carte blanche. The art Goddess took what was there, melding with it parts she drew from her own palette. It is as if she brought the environment in better focus, heightened energies by freeing their potential – all by grafting her creational skills onto those of the host Goddess. GG- Enola is turning the battle energy of her native self, into the dynamic forces of visual arts – all of us involved bear witness to it.

"The anticipation of evil in the human heart is at the root of all wars," she says. "It is the vortex that draws the powers of the creator into the hands of the destroyer. The energy remains the same – unpolarized. What is polarized is the thinking that claims its ownership for the purpose of gain and control, or, at the other end, the impulse that draws one to arrange flowers or write a poem. Fire can ravage a forest, or bring comfort to the body on a cold night – energy doesn't discriminate."

We, Angels, of course live by it, but the visual expression of those principles applied with such skills is a sight to behold – though it would be unfair to limit GG-Enola's talents to only what the eye can see.

Angel Lev is from the open-ended school of spontaneous arts, where and when space and moment play the critical parts of the expressers via the insertion of an unrelated external activator – preferably one that disappears in the statement. His talents are amply present in countless subtle nuances – to great effect.

"Everything is art that begs to be noticed," he says with distinct amusement.

On this very subject, one may say that the villagers of Xarn's realm befit the expression – though in a uniquely dignified way. Their genetic makeup, as per Angel Monique, is the result of math turned to shapes and colors as if it were – metaphorically speaking – the work of the *Mandelbrot set*, which puts G-God Xarn, the creator, in a league all of his own.

It is very difficult to accurately describe the mien of these endearing creatures. Their common strain is expressed in the form of "collective goodness," as if an invisible strand of DNA connected them all into one single gestalt. Yet, each of them represents a unique variation on the marriage of species, in ways never seen before across the entire physical plane of our original Oneness. Their outer covers can be skin, scales, feather, or fur, with predominant tones leaning towards greens, blues, and reds in various graphic arrangements. At the humanoid end, they display the standard characteristics of the race – except for pigmentation – while as the genes veer off towards the exotic, billed quadrupeds easily mix with winged flightless mammals. Their sizes are remarkably within proportion of each other. For the rest, I must let your imagination do the work, for wherever it takes you – you will never be too far from reality.

17 – EARLY DAY IN THE GREAT HALL

Place of activity: The New Guild Center
Date: year 1 of the Realms, G-day 1
Chronicler: Senior Master Qo'ai-Marael,
Honorary member Department of
Warrior and Realm History

———————

While in-body, everyone needs sleep – Angels or not. That is the way the physical stays in touch with the spiritual – through dreams and *bio-auratic* channels. While I favor an early rise and the sight of an auspicious dawn, others like to take advantage of the benefits of sleep, and thus allow for those such as myself, the enjoyment of a relatively quiet Hall. Apparently, Master Jaco isn't among that late group, as he moves at a brisk pace towards me.

"Nothing like thinking room," he says.

I can't help myself from asking what he thinks about.

"It's metaphorical; I enjoy pointless humor. How's your morning so far?" he asks.

"Recording an uneventful moment in the history of the realms, if you should know," I respond.

I am not sure it was my intention to put it in such blunt terms, but he nods and moves on. The passing of time isn't a quantifier generally recognized by Angels, but in the case of Jaco, the millennia since we worked together have vividly affected my perception of his character – we both are changed by directions that take us further apart. I sense that since the Battles, he has sought isolation from mainstream with the purpose of hiding his discontentment towards the choice of helping the tribes. His presence here worries me, yet I do not recognize the reason why it should. It's quite possible Angel Jaco, as well as most of the other elders, are here to embrace the fact they were once misled by their passions. There is no better test of character than facing one's demons, even for an Angel – no pun intended.

It is now Master Lo-shen's time to come and greet me from a few paces away. She looks radiant, youthful, fit, though her aura doesn't try to conceal her seniority. Back in the pre-eras of the Great Battles, she was the coalescing force behind the divisions of the league; the one who forged alliances into what would become the Guild. Her name is all over history. She too vanished from the face of reality after the Battles and the "sowing" of the realms. Nothing is recorded of her from that point on. It is thought she went on a sabbatical.

"Like-minds," she says smiling warmly.

I smile back as we hug.

"Looking for Angel Jaco?" I ask.

"More like arranging to bump into him," she humors.

"I believe he did just that with me a moment ago," I humor back.

She takes my arm and invites me to walk along.

"Since we seem to be on the same page," she says, "I'm going to be frank – I need to know what Master Jaco says or where he goes when I'm not around. Would you care sharing what you may be aware of, as well as your thoughts regarding his movements and connections?"

I am taken aback by the request. What kind of Angel in her right mind would put forth such a question? I keep silent for a moment that may be too long for the Master.

"Never mind," she says, as if to try to reassure me, "it's not that important."

"He and I are from Amaterasu and Vac's original team, before the rescue of young Joonas. I cannot, for the life of me, honor your request without breaking a fundamental tenet of our code of ethics. What went down later doesn't change my allegiance to what bonded us then – I'm sorry," I hear myself say, somewhat confused.

"I'm the one who's sorry," she returns.

We walk to the cafeteria where Jaco is seen with Angels Rashnu, Niamh, and Theyia. Lo-shen lets go of my arm and asks if I want to join. I decline politely by requesting a rain check.

"What about tomorrow – same time?" she tentatively offers, smiling as if to seek forgiveness.

I acquiesce with the knowledge that I'm setting myself up for something I'm uncertain I want to be part of. I now wonder what role Master Lo-shen is playing, in what is now becoming something larger than the sum of its parts. I only wish those parts and that whole had definers.

18 – KITCHEN AFFAIRS

Place of action: Great Goddess Ma-l's domain
Date: year 1 of the Ma-lean calendar, G-day 1
Chronicler: Angel Vera, team Le Lien,
Guild archivist

Not only was it a long night shift, but now Ma-l calls for a meeting at the crack of dawn. I don't need much sleep – but sorry – one hour is just a tease. Anyway, nothing coffee can't fix!

OK, everyone's here, Saka, Marshall, Geir, Lillian, Olaf, Pau, Liv, Vac and Sam, Bluefeather as the proverbial wild card, Xarn, Enola, plus Lev and Gretchen. I don't see Shade and Shido, but I can't blame them for their absence – they did more than their share by helping Pau get the gig with Marshall. The crews of volunteers aren't due for another Ma-lean hour; additionally, Goddess Enola tells us the performers are not showing up until later in the morning. It means no chaos while things get organized. Amaterasu makes a brief appearance to give everyone her blessings – she promises to weave in and out for the length of the gathering.

While Ma-l and the two Warriors go over realm coordination, Vac takes Lillian, Liv, and me to the side to give us the lowdown on how to keep an eye on the elders, while looking for clues as to their true reasons to be among us. He tells us Angel Grisha will assist with updates from

Hall portals and that it can't hurt to hear what Master Khaldun has to say – he may home on defining nuances.

We regroup around catering matters: all-day buffets to be replenished, dishes – the works. I think we all know what to do, so the Goddess can take care of her Goddess things. Ma-l gets the point then wishes us good luck. She's not going anywhere though – it's her party – she's in it for the stretch. Olaf tells me that while we were sleeping – *expletive duly deleted* – she went to visit Snake at the crater to make sure all was a go with the bonfires – Snake is delivering as promised. It's my understanding Ma-l has a soft spot for the mighty elemental entity; thus, she wants to make sure it is loved the proper way – a Goddess' work knows no bounds.

Xarn returns to his realm to prepare his people for the crossing. He must teach them the use of portals as well as the doors in Joonas Halls. Saka stays with Ma-l.

I zoom on Sam for a second – I pick something unusual about him. I know dogs from my many Earth assignments – this one's curiously different though. I wonder if Vac's influence has anything to do with it.

Lillian and Geir are flirting with each other, while pretending to pay attention to last-minute instructions, but it doesn't escape Bluefeather's colorful mind – got to love him for staying focused on the job!

Oh my poor head, I need more coffee!

OK, I'm back and coherent! I just needed a fix and a break from the triple assignment. I always seem to take more than I can chew – I guess it goes with my nature, which is kind of random in a quasi-organized sort of way.

I'm not sure whether talking about my eccentricities adds fodder to the chronicling or not, but I guess that's why we have editing.

Just in case some of you are unfamiliar with the way we, Angels, communicate: it's done on a réseau of telepathic private lines. It's intuitive, requires permission and it's unhackable – it also works in conference mode. So when Angel Grisha has something for Lillian, Liv, and me, we can all tune in. A skilled Master could potentially break into an existing communication, but not without revealing their presence, identity, and motives – which is a straight connection to Le Lien's surveillance apparatus. It never occurs.

So when Grisha wants to let us know Masters Caax and Dzalarhons are in the process of accessing Goddess Enola's realms, while she's here working on preparations, all he needs to do is recall the particular code of the contract between parties to activate the conversation. It's not strictly a mental thing – it happens on multiple levels outside the self too – similar to finding ourselves in the same room within a parallel layer of consciousness – you get the idea. Of course, the three of us are quick to inform the Goddess of the elders' intentions, so she excuses herself while she readies her core consciousness for the duty of being in more than one place at once. She thanks us.

It goes without saying that Dzalarhons and Caax are well informed that Enola's realm is temporary off-limit. Angel Gretchen is seen rushing back there, so we may get the lowdown on how the two elders' maneuver is received. It's the second intrusion I hear of. Monique reported one in Xarn's world two days ago. We have a female elder, but no name, who tampered with portal codes to top it all!

I've got to wonder how much these Masters are actually flirting with protocol for the sake of letting everyone know that they are – to the point that it's becoming less obvious whether it is intentional or not. Are they playing on the ticket of their long absences, or are they just being oblivious from not having adapted to the inevitable changes of Guild evolution? When in doubt, remember we're dealing with Masters – there is no such thing as them being clueless. The way my mind wanders, it takes me straight to a planned diversion. I share my thoughts on a separate line reserved for Le Lien data input, which can also be accessed by Liv, Lillian, and Spencer.

The whole thing could be a farce played by the variables of a new Oneness – a mishap in perception while the sensors go through their calibration process. We haven't, to this point, dealt with powerful outside elements against which to pit our adjusted perspectives – the elders still ride on the winds of the original Oneness, propelled by the momentum of their seniority.

The one thing that sticks out of this whole charade is the sense of confusion that is being spread around. That's the crux of it; its origin must be defined separately from the trigger – Le Lien lets me know I'm onto something.

I'm aware this chronicling is veering off tangentially, but context rules. Angel Gretchen always says that there's no painting without a canvas – though I can already hear the voice of objection. The way I see it, background defines the mood of a gathering worthy of the name.

19 – PORTALS TO THE GATHERING

Places of action: the Great Hall and Ma-l's realm
Date: year 1 of the Realms, G-day 1
Chronicler: Angel Grisha
Department of Warrior and Realm History

In anticipation of the large attendance, several portals have been linked together from various areas of the Great Hall. I wish it were otherwise since I am being asked to monitor crossing activity. I have strategically placed my personal accesses to maximize the scope of my chronicling, but there is no way I can be in more than one place simultaneously – at least not in-body.

It is still early morning in the New Guild Center, so it's relatively easy to go from point to point without missing much of the action. I see elder Qo'ai-Marael arm in arm with Master Lo-shen; a minute ago, it was Angel Jaco who brushed by me with only the slightest of acknowledgement. It appears our previous interaction has somewhat marginalized my presence in the Master's arc of perception.

It is no surprise that the majority of the early risers are elders; though again, for the non-Angels among our readers, their looks can be quite deceptive.

After yesterday's cafeteria incident, I chose to let Vac know that I would honor his request. I found him in conversation with Angel Spencer, who introduced himself as a member of team Le Lien of interdimensional surveillance. I now grasp the seriousness of what's being asked of me. It is somewhat fitting that I should find myself in the settings of intrigue after having documented so much of it through my research, though I am quite confident the office environment of the department doesn't make me an automatic qualifier for this type of field work. The active act of reporting, should one find themselves amidst events of recordable value, is part of making history – a dream come true for any historian with an avid conspirative mind.

Agent Spencer connects me with Angels Liv, Lillian, and Vera who are stationed on Goddess Ma-l's celebratory grounds – the aim is for me to inform them of realm-bound elder traffic.

It just so happens that at this very moment, on floor twenty-seven of stairwell four, Masters Caax and Dzalarhons approach the entrance of the tunnel that leads to Great Goddess Enola's domain then vanish inside it. There is no hesitation on their part, no slowing down; they could easily be mistaken for two souls late for a meeting. The act would be inconsequential if it weren't for the fact Enola's realm is strictly off-limit this morning. No doubt they knew about it before they went ahead – I notify the team.

Portals and the stone tunnels between the Hall and the realms are not monitored, and based on a set agreement between the three Warriors, Great One Amaterasu, and the Assembly, they never will be. The reason is simple: this new Oneness belongs to the Goddesses and Gods of the realms – their lanes must remain open to allow for the rising worlds to merge with the whole. In other words, they are vital arteries, vulnerable only to outside forces which technically have been non-existent since the demise of

Hektor. Amaterasu's throughway between the stones is off-limit to any signature that doesn't resonate harmonically with the fundamental pitch of the collective realms – but apparently something went wrong. It is why I stand here with a tablet connected to the history department's database on one hand, and a private line to three of the Le Lien team on the other. It somehow reminds me of my last assignment in the old Soviet Union of Earth, as I stood in the freezing weather with my subject, endlessly waiting for obscure connections. His name was Mikhail – he always asked for favors. Unfortunately, I couldn't save him from himself.

There are around one hundred elders, though I only know a few I can spot from a distance. Hopefully, there won't be any more foul play. Xarn's realm is closed-off to visitors and guarded at his end; I suspect Enola will take measures as well. It leaves Ma-l's which is technically open to all via multiple temporary portals. I just have to take it in stride.

I pass Masters Jaco, Rashnu, and Niamh as they leave the cafeteria. Angel Lo-shen is in conversation with Theyia inside – I wave. I pick up my Russian Caravan to-go, ready to exit when I am called to their table.

"Looking forward to celebrating?" Theyia asks.

I greet the both of them.

"I celebrate the emergence of the Oneness in a way that suits best my person – I document," I reply.

"Aren't you on the wrong side of the portals for that?" she counters.

Master Lo-shen interrupts.

"Angel Grisha is of course in charge of providing a backdrop account of the event."

"I am indeed – no stones left unturned," I add, turning briefly to Master Theyia.

"I don't want to take you away from your work, Grisha, but let's please connect when you find the time. I must know more about some specific details of realm history," Lo-shen says.

"Perhaps in the next few days," I reply.

I leave the pair to return to my assignment.

Call it intuitive on my part, but I have one of my own portals set at the old entrance to Goddess Ma-l's realm – the one on top of the third stairwell. It is where I go from the cafeteria. It's well known the passageway is blocked at its end, and only the Goddess can travel through it by borrowing part of the tunnel into Snake's underworld. It is also lesser known that the lane once connected with the now-frozen maze previously controlled by Gestalt George, also where Joonas was last seen by Angel Vac.

I am looking down at the majesty of the Great Hall, when elder Jaco surprises me with his presence.

"So, Angel Grisha, enjoying a bit of quietude before the floor comes to life?"

"It is one way to put it, Master Jaco, but I'm also positioning my work portals strategically with those accessing Great Goddess Ma-l's realm. This one is of course of no consequence to visitors, but it is to me, as one of the historians who documented its use in the original version of Angel City," I explain.

"It is my understanding that you wouldn't be here if you didn't expect the adventurous of mind to dare a more unique entrance into the Warrior's world," Jaco probes.

"You are reading me accurately; as you can see, it pays off," I return with humor.

"Indeed Angel, it doesn't escape me that you are bound to your work by the forces of loyalty and commitment – something I appreciate in my kin. But please explain why it would matter if anyone tried to visit these tunnels – as far as I know, they aren't off-limit."

"You are absolutely right, it doesn't matter, Master Jaco. I am sure you understand I'm here as part of covering all angles; such is the task to be in charge of documenting traffic to Great Goddess Ma-l's celebration."

"Of course it is, Angel, but you are only partially answering my question – perhaps I should come to the point: why are you asked to do a headcount on this side of the portals when it could just as easily be done at the other end? And who's behind the request?" Jaco inquires.

I feel I'm being probed, but there is no turning around – I sense he already knows.

"It is asked of me that I monitor unusual activity on this side of the various entrances into the Warrior's realms – not just Ma-l's. It's an extra, minor assignment attached to my chronicling of the peripheral aspects of the event. As to the source of the request, I am not at liberty to tell."

"You understand I have seniority that begs for my questions to be answered without reserve, Angel?"

"I can only answer by reminding you that in regard to this Oneness, my seniority precedes yours. The New Guild Center is the only authority we both serve; I believe you knew that before you made your choice, Angel Jaco."

"Indeed, Grisha," the Master responds in a softer tone, "my apologies for portraying myself as inquisitive – the newness of it brings forth much curiosity that is received with few answers. I'm still very much old-school, as you certainly know – the most challenging part of experience is to let go of old habits."

I let him know that no offense is taken. For the first time since we met, I feel an element of common decency in our interaction. He asks if he may borrow my portal to get to the floor – I oblige.

"Ad conventum," he says, on his way down.

20 – DZALARHONS & CAAX'S VISIT

Place: Great Goddess Enola's domain
Date: year 1 of the Enolaean calendar, G-day 1
Chronicler: Angel Gretchen
Department of Warrior and Realm History

As soon as I hear the news about the intrusion, I catch the nearest portal to GG-Enola's domain. While the Goddess remains in Ma-l's world with the crew, her core consciousness technically never leaves her realm – the Warrior is there to receive the errant visitors.

It first must be said that in agreement with G-God Xarn, a group of his villagers volunteered to stay in the colorful city while Enola, Lev, and I worked on GG-Ma-l's festivity grounds. Angel Monique believes Xarn's species perfectly match GG-Enola's creation – I agree, but only to a point, due to vast differences between the two Warriors.

Also, unlike the original entries into realms one and two, with one overlooking a widening valley, while the other sits atop a deep canyon, the access into Enola's world is through one of the gates of her city – carved into the face of a purplish-red rocky mound at the north end of town. Beyond the lone protrusion, stretches a wide, flat desert that meets with high mountains in the distance.

When Masters Dzalarhons and Caax arrive, they are first met by the group of G-God Xarn's villagers – I quickly join them, but GG-Enola is nowhere in sight.

The two Angels look at us curiously, as if to evaluate the evolutionary marker of the specimens they are facing. My presence seems to put them at ease.

"Ah, Angel, perhaps you can point to the places of interest," Caax says, somewhat arrogantly.

"You've just found one of them, Master; regrettably it goes no further."

"I assume you and your gang of beasts have the authority to make such an assessment," Dzalarhons lashes.

"I have the authority to remind you that it is protocol to follow portal recommendation. For the time being, this realm is off-limit – I believe you two knew that already."

The villagers look oddly fascinated. Skatu, Alice, and Jessie have been exposed to Goddesses and Angels alike, but the other four show puzzlement. It is my guess none of them recognizes the energy emanating from the two Masters. Their gentleness is unaccustomed to the intruders' aggressive behavior – it is a quality alien to them.

We appear to be at a standstill. I don't comprehend the position of the two elders, and why they wished to forcefully engage.

GG-Enola comes through the opening behind them, blocking its entrance. She radiates with the energy of her Warrior self – stealthy and ready to strike.

"Turn around, Angels!" she calls.

It rings like a final order – the two Masters show surprise. Now, with their backs to the group, they must face the true authority of the world they just trespassed upon.

"Amongst the many individuals I have met since the inception of my realm, not a single one is capable of challenging the soundness of my wish and disregarding the sacrosanctity of my city; yet, based on your presence and the words with which you described my guests, you two appear to be doing both with utmost impunity. I have no doubts you are from among those we call the elders. Paradoxically, your lack of wisdom betrays the deep divisions of your Guild – I shall make sure you are sent back wherefrom you came. My stand is not negotiable – consider yourself in my custody until I arrange for your removal."

Dzalarhons and Caax advance menacingly towards the Goddess.

"Without us, you wouldn't be here, Warrior," the female Master spits.

"And without me, neither would you, Angel – know your place!" Enola returns with ice in her voice.

With that, the immediate physicality of the intruders turns into a thin vibrational field. Their attempts to free themselves from it only lead to tightening the snare.

"They're not going anywhere," GG-Enola tells me.

The villagers and I are utterly mesmerized by what is just happening. The Goddess of art and harmony – short of resorting to the use of arrows – is momentarily, I only hope, reconnecting with her Warrior self. This is bound to create a stir in the Great Hall. I connect with Angel Vera with whom I have a private line.

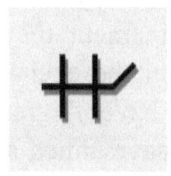

21 – THE ENOLA DILEMMA

Places of action: Great Goddesses Ma-l's domain and Enola's tunnel from the Great Hall
Date: year 1 of the realms, G-day 1
Chronicler: Angel Vera, team Le Lien,
Guild archivist

I receive Angel Gretchen's message – I can't believe my eyes. I contact Le Lien. Within barely a minute, Vac and Amaterasu are in conversation with the part of Enola in charge of décor.

For the non-Angels out there, Enola is Enola whether she is one or two, or on both sides of the fence. Regardless of how many selves she projects, her core identity will always remain in her realm – she is her realm, physically and beyond. The same goes for Ma-l and Xarn.

I telepathically ask permission from Vac and the Great One to get in on the conversation – permission granted.

What transpires is that the two Masters showed pointed disregard to Angel Gretchen and the villagers. They also moved threateningly towards the Goddess, which thus explains the confinement they are now in. Liv and Spencer soon join in on the exchange. It is irrefutable – Dzalarhons and Caax have flagrantly violated protocol. Without a doubt, they have aimed at creating a diplomatic vacuum with the possible consequences of jeopardizing the gathering, the integrity of the merging of the three open realms, as well as the future of the still-dormant worlds. It is an act of sabotage at the highest level that must urgently be dealt with.

The festivities will go on as planned. Enola is fine with Le Lien transferring the trespassers to the Great Hall security unit. Vac connects with Qo'ai-Marael for the scheduling of a behind-closed-door emergency meeting set for the following day, with the six most senior Masters of Angel City – no explanation given. Pending reached consensus, all late-arrival elders are to be screened for possible extradition. Until then, nothing must transpire or be mentioned that could alert the suspects.

Talk about a tight rope act.

Here's the scoop: no-one beyond Le Lien, Vac, Gretchen, Enola, Amaterasu, Qo'ai-Marael, and the meeting seniors, must know about what's going on – not even Ma-l, Olaf, Saka, and Xarn. Hopefully the villagers present at the arrest will remain silent.

———————

It's now midday – the place is getting packed. Performances are in progress on multiple stages, while food and drinks are served from a dozen student-operated buffets. The kitchen is in full rotation, and will be so for the length of the festival.

I'm still hoping to escape with Bluefeather – too much work without fun is bound to make an Angel moody – and definitely less efficient! Lillian's on the team – I'm certain she agrees.

It's a good thing the Great Hall needs to maintain

its day-to-day operation, because I don't know where we would put all these Angels. So far, I've not yet seen any of the elders, beyond Master Emile who came in to entertain the kitchen, and Lo-shen, who walked in briefly to charm me. I know she's *Third Eye* but she won't tell. I hope I'm right – we could use the help of a mysterious benefactor. I let Le Lien know of my intuition – Spencer is puzzled at the suggestion.

"We are what *Third Eye* used to be – they're long gone," he says.

But he knows what I think and that troubles him.

Dzalarhons and Caax are now locked in Le Lien's security unit. They obviously chose to take one for the team – but what team, and to what ultimate aim? It makes zero sense. The trespassing alone is a minor offence that doesn't warrant an arrest, but provocation is over the top for Angels. It smells of fabrication meant to serve someone who wants to see the realms fail; but with Joonas and Hektor gone, Le Lien is left with a blank slate. I suggest one of us returns to Guild Headquarters to sift through communication and portal archives, to look for connections between Hektor and elder Masters. We had assumed Tömör was the only traitor – but what about all those who reversed their positions when the notion of losing Guild privileges hit them with a dose of reality? It makes some sort of sense that a group of Masters not seen for eons – then spontaneously appearing in one extremely unique area of existence – would eventually have something to show for it. And why would Caax and Dzalarhons use the tunnels? Was it their intention to get to Enola's place, or were they snooping around the corridors for other purposes? It hits me that I might be onto something. I tell Spencer – he agrees.

I ask for relief from kitchen duty and to be given

clearance to retrace the rogue Angels' steps with Enola. Both Le Lien and the Great Goddess are for it. Spencer demands I keep it short and sweet.

———————

Enola and I arrive at twenty-seven and three via private portal – no-one sees us. We enter the tunnel which is first lined with a series of rooms, before it tapers to a narrow passage. The Great Goddess turns herself into a guiding light – we stay in telepathic mode. The plan is not to go directly to her realm since it serves no real purpose, but to find whatever portal is integral to the tunnel that only the Warrior can access. I suggest she thinks of a destination, such as Snake's underworld. It must be working, because we descend a long twisting corridor until it flattens and gives way, not to a crater, but to Xarn's plateau above the canyon – Wolf is right there before us.

"What brings you here?" he asks, uncertain of what should be done next.

"Not to worry, Wolf, we're only peeking – we must have made the wrong turn and landed here. It wasn't our intention," Enola explains. "But before we go, did your intruder come this way as well?"

"She most certainly did," the coywolf replies.

"Please tell no-one of our visit; it's important it stays between us," the Goddess requested.

"Will do – let me know when you decide to populate your realm, I may have ideas."

Enola laughs.

"It's a deal, Wolf," she promises.

We turn around and reenter the rock face.

22 – FROM THE FLOOR & THE CAFETERIA

Place of activity: The New Guild Center
Date: year 1 of the Realms, G-day 1 & 2
Chronicler: Senior Master Qo'ai-Marael,
Honorary member Department of
Warrior and Realm History

THE FLOOR

I am trying to wrap my head around Angel Vac's notification: an emergency meeting expressively sought by Great One Amaterasu. I am given no explanation, aside from the fact it will be conducted behind closed doors. My presentiment is that the gathering must not be disrupted, for I am requested to keep the information to myself under the rarely-used code of secrecy, *hic solum*. Indeed, the only other such meeting since the time of the Great Battles was around the Tömör treason case.

I am somewhat concerned this may have to do with some of my old friends who have been acting rather oddly since their arrival. Master Jaco's dark energy, Angel Loshen unusual request, elder Dzalarhons inexplicable distrust of my words... It did not hit me as peculiar at first, but the exacerbating effect of their behavior now resonates with a distinct dissonance. There seems to be calculated confusion at play in the form of "planned randomness."

There is also an aura of division between some of them that may only exist for the further purpose of disorientation – the effect is one of smoke and mirrors.

I promised Master Lo-shen I would join her for an early breakfast tomorrow; perhaps light can be shed from her end.

For now, I am connecting with guests returning from Ma-l's grand gathering, who are telling me how delighted they are to be partaking in this extraordinary historic moment. The grounds are teeming with the multitudes under the auspices of harmony and joy. Everything, from the décor to the food and performances, is beyond expectation. For the many who must return to their work, there is the promise of many more days ahead – indeed, no-one wishes for it to end prematurely.

THE CAFETERIA

As expected, Master Lo-shen is already waiting at one of the cafeteria tables, but so are Angels Jaco and Tealsky. I am not sure I am prepared to socialize at their level, considering the differences that have grown between us since the olden days.

I apologize for my slight lateness to which I receive the customary "please don't." I sit in between the two females, facing Jaco who gives me a corner smile.

"Glad you could join us, Master Qo'ai-Marael; there are quite a few things we are struggling with in the furthering of our education – perhaps you're in a position to help us with it," Angel Tealsky said.

"I shall do my best," I reply, "but keep in mind much has changed since we last worked together – now with the emerging Oneness, many of the old rules no longer apply."

"You may elucidate on the last item – isn't the Guild bound to its own guidelines regardless of which side it operates from?" Jaco asks.

"Let me first clarify that here, Guild guidelines honor the wish of the Warriors in exactly the same way they do the ones of the many civilizations we see rise and fall in the Oneness from which we come. The one major difference is that in this place, we work together as opposed to behind the scene. We have made the choice of serving the realms; therefore we are committed to it. If that is not clear to you, I advise you rethink your reasons for being here. Secondly, seniority means nothing in this universe, since we all start from the same platform; it's a new birth, literally. And a most important third: we did not come here with our previous crippling divisions. This assembly operates as one and I regret it may be poorly understood amongst some in your group. I am sorry for the bluntness," I explain with some discomfort.

"I am confused about the way you see this emergence – is it not the result of the work of Angels?" Tealsky asks coldly.

"Master Jaco and I were part of the original team long before Angel Lo-shen here, as well as many elders such as yourself, helped consolidate numerous loose factions of disoriented young Angels into the Guild. As we traveled the light to the farthest probabilities, we saw a glimpse of what *could* become the realms. It was faint but it held potentiality. We did not create the event. Now, when came the time to assist the tribes and free the Warriors, I do not recollect any of you being around to help. As a matter of fact, some vehemently opposed the Great Ones' request, making a point of taking the farthest assignments as an expression of their discontentment. And now you have returned to claim your place as if it were a deeded right, I assume," I reply, amazed at my own response.

"Blunt to say the least, Master," Jaco says, "but I appreciate that in you – now I remember why we worked together well. That being said, you are correct – I did not agree with the Guild's choice to take on the Great Ones' project and I spoke loudly about it. I admired Joonas, but he was too much of a loose cannon for me; plus, he reminded me of the cankerous humans. I chose to be forgotten out of disgust, not discontentment – the whole thing troubled me deeply. But now that I am here, I can see I was wrong not to trust the Ones and the Angels who chose to work for them. It's a hard lesson which at times, leaves me bitter about my own lack of foresight – I bear my own cross and hopefully, I'm here to let go of it."

"I did not expect such a confession from you, Master; you have my deepest respect," I say, uncertain I heard him right.

Angel Lo-shen, with whom I originally was set to meet, has not said a thing yet. She simply observes as if to store data for further review.

Master Tealsky does not appear impressed – she may perceive Jaco's explanation as a betrayal.

"The way I hear it, Qo'ai-Marael, comparing my choice of volunteering my skills for the benefit of the realms and the advancement of the Guild, to insinuating I am here to fetch my slice of the pie, is at best insolent. How do you come to such conclusion, if I may ask?"

"Insolence is a term that enjoys bouncing back to its

86

point of origin, Angel. This place welcomes you with open arms, yet from day one, you and many of our old friends have been inquisitive, openly aggressive, and mean-spirited. Your collective behavior has been quite perplexing to say the least."

Master Lo-shen finally cuts in.

"I invited Master Qo'ai-Marael for a pleasant conversation. I did not expect it would come to these terms. Please, let us compose ourselves and act like Angels worthy of the name."

Master Tealsky got up, nodded and left.

"I can see you two are clear," Lo-shen says, "but there is trouble on the horizon. Master Jaco, welcome back to the fold!"

Jaco smiles a real smile for the first time since he arrived.

I am at a loss as to what is just happening – in what capacity exactly, is Master Lo-shen acting?

As if she is reading my thoughts, she turns to me and says, "I believe you have a busy day ahead of you, but by its end, all will become clear."

We stand as one and part with few words. A weight lifts while another takes its place.

23 – THE ARREST

Areas of activity: Warrior Enola's realm & Le Lien
Headquarters
Date: year 1 of the Realms, G-day 2
Chronicler: Angel Spencer, team Le Lien

By the time of the publishing of the chronicles of this grand celebration, it is hoped that all unsettling matters will be resolved. Though I am not one of the reporters, it is my wish, in view of my position at Le Lien, that my input should contribute a layer of transparency to these unexpected developments.

Technically speaking, Masters Dzalarhons and Caax committed the acts of trespassing, insulting a native species, as well as threatening a Goddess of the realms, on the suspicion of creating a planned disruption, under yet-to-be-determined motives.

The presence of Angel Gretchen as witness, brings the case within the active periphery of our jurisdiction, if permitted by representatives of the land. In this instance, Warrior Enola, as the official voice of her realm, agrees to hand the case over to New Guild Center security.

From my perspective, it's quite conceivable that the intruding Masters did not anticipate the company of an outside witness; hence, erroneously acting on momentum – they are now in our custody.

We are able to determine that the site of the

infraction is consistent with the use of the second system of tunnels put in place before Joonas Halls. Said system technically connects all realms to each other via the Great Hall, but Warriors have access to integral markers and portals specifically designed to recognize their unique signatures, and thus can bypass the hub. Such throughways are inherently off-limit to all.

This second version is a duplicate of the original corridors once controlled by rogue gestalt, George. Both systems are linked via Snake's underworld and the arrested realms, but these paths were made off-limit following the migration from Angel City to the New Guild Center, and the subsequent demise of the gestalt. The old tunnels are now technically dead.

As per yesterday's authorized request, Warrior Enola and Master Vera have been retracing Dzalarhons and Caax's steps, for the purpose of isolating possible clues as to why they chose that route instead of the more public access via Joonas Halls. I am awaiting their report.

When we arrested the trespassers, we found them shrouded in a force field of alien technology. A sample of the readout was sent to Qwave labs. It is clear Warrior Enola's skills reach far beyond the creations she is known for. It is well noted that breaches in protocol are matters of particular sensitivity to these deities, leading to responses that are swift and highly efficient; and in this case, apparently not negotiable.

There was also a report of attempted transgression from guidelines in Warrior Xarn's realm on day -2. The Angel was not identified, but we believe she was from the same group as our detainees.

There is a closed meeting tonight regarding both incidents and their ties to the latest arrival of elders. A panel of judges will be assembled for Dzalarhons and Caax's trial. It is said Great One Amaterasu will preside. I shall be there as representative of *Guild and Realm Affairs*. To my great surprise, Vac informed me that Masters Jaco and Lo-shen would also be attending in a capacity that is not to be confirmed until "due time." Considering the importance of the matter, I applaud the decision, as it is only fair that members of their group be present, even if Master Jaco's manners have raised concerns with alarming regularity.

For the time being, no-one has come forward to inquire about the whereabouts of the two detained Angels. It opens the field to speculation, since Dzalarhons and Caax were seen daily in the presence of at least one of the following elders: Niamh, Tealsky, Theyia, Rashnu, and Emile. At the exception of the latter, each has been the subject of complaints varying from minor to serious, mostly about ignored etiquette. The silence around the arrest could signify that – from my subjective perspective – the outcome of their stunt was expected. I am not at liberty to use my personal views to incriminate anyone, but this is not a security report. I do hope these words will add intrigue to the background of the celebration, and that by being included in the final draft – probability permitting – they will point to a propitious outcome.

24 – ENOLA'S TUNNELS

Place of action: Great Goddesses Enola's tunnel
Date: year 1 of the realms, G-day 1 & 2
Chronicler: Angel Vera, team Le Lien,
Guild archivist

―――――――――

Enola and I reenter the tunnel from Xarn's place. We trust Wolf won't spread the word of our brief visit. It's my first time crossing over from one realm to another without using one of the two hubs. To make sure we haven't gone astray, the Goddess brings us back to the northern gate of her city – and in, we go again.

I haven't to this point brought up what has been on my mind from the get-go – mostly because of its outrageousness – but I'll be frank: I suspect these Masters, among other reasons for snooping around, are also looking for a way to get to Joonas. I don't have the foggiest idea of how these chronicles will be arranged at publishing time, or how much of them will be edited out, but perhaps the reader already knows where I'm coming from – just a hunch.

Anyway, Enola and I – which means me following the Goddess – are in the process of locating a marker for Snake's underworld, which we believe will allow us to come to the old throughways into the original maze of tunnels. Now, let me be clear – Snake's world is accessible via the New Guild Center and has been for the longest time through the backdoor of Ma-l's domain at the top of her valley – but it has never been reached from either Enola or Xarn's tunnel. So this is a first.

Another point of importance is that all entrances into the developmentally arrested realms have been linked by Snake during the carving of the new tunnels even though they are missing from Joonas Halls.

When George was deleted, the old system of lanes became inoperative, but accesses to the failed realities remained unchanged – probably because the codes had already deteriorated before the gestalt ever thought of closing the ways to these aborted realms.

I believe we're now on the same page.

I'm saying this because we arrive at the back of a cave occupied by a ghost Warrior – I think he's some sort of hologram left over from spatial memory. The odd thing is, he knows of our presence and wants us to leave, while simultaneously wishing for us to rot in hell – nice guy.

On our second try, we end up in yet another cave lined with dusty altars littered with fragile artifacts – mostly twigs, bones, and small crude clay figures. There's a faint glow to it, but that's all which is left of the Warrior. Enola feels sadness at the loss of these realms. It's likely that when she spoke with Ma-1 about them, she didn't anticipate how deep their failures would be felt firsthand. I sympathize, but nothing more.

Enola and I are not exactly sisters – we don't know each other. We break the ice slowly, but I can tell she's some intense female. How she snared those two intruders is classic Warrior stuff. In other words, don't fuck with her – I so relate. Incidentally, the way we warm up to each other is by talking about her battle days – it wasn't all peachy keen then. Analytically speaking, the cheerfulness of her art is in direct contrast with the pain inflicted by tribal demands forced onto her psyche at a young age – she simply had no choice. The repressed creativity is what made her fierce; obviously that fierceness didn't totally leave her, in spite of the arts and all. The same could be said of Ma-l and Xarn – I have no doubts about it. I heard it from Vac that his initial entry into the realms with Olaf wasn't exactly received with kindness. It's just as well for Hektor that they are enjoying their gifted universe – but once again, I digress.

After yet another failed approach to Snake's domain and the obligatory cave – this time, with random angry utterances aimed at hypothetical menaces, bouncing from wall to wall like mad ping-pong balls – we decide that perhaps the fire gestalt doesn't want to be bothered, or is too busy with its role at the celebration. It's obvious Enola is not presently on its guest list.

I suggest that since the tunnels to the aborted realms once provided corridors between Angel City and the New Guild Center – though only Snake's was used for that purpose because of its connection to Ma-l's domain – they all must still conceal trace markers to the old Hall. Enola reminds me that she was there and I wasn't, while begging of me to please stop stating the obvious. Point well taken.

She also refreshes my memory on Joonas's involvement with the deletion of the rogue gestalt, and on the fact the markers were erased as well – but then, how did Vac get out, and what are we looking for?

"Angel Vera," she says, "the erasure of the markers was gradual; now you look for clues that align with your skills, while I work on locating the old lanes. Can we stick to that and not get in each other's way?"

Ouch! Here I go again – cross-tasking when I could just be minding my own business.

"Sorry," I simply say.

I must return to my center of gravity. For that, I shut my thoughts and let my surroundings do the talking.

That's when I notice what I was originally looking for, but didn't know what it was then: a seed algorithm freshly embedded in the stone right at mid-distance from the last cave and its connecting point into Enola's tunnel – we, at Le Lien, train for that sort of thing! I take a reading with my trusty tablet scanner then try to send the data to headquarters – it doesn't want to connect. We're either too deep or the timelines have shifted.

I show my findings to Enola – they puzzle her.

"I don't like the look of it, Vera. The way I see it, this thing migrated here – there's no Angel signature in the vicinity, but there's a ghost image of the seed that fades back towards its point of origin. Thank you, and my apologies, I wouldn't have noticed without you! I believe this seed knows were it belongs; therefore it found its own way from my tunnel. This is the exact placement of the old marker; a new one is replacing it, tapping the energy of its predecessor and copying its characteristics. Someone is trying to clone George," Enola telepathically shares.

I agree – this is bad news. I'm almost certain the same happened inside Xarn and Ma-l's tunnels. I must return to Le Lien headquarters immediately. My, how long have we been in this maze? I suddenly realize much time has passed since we entered it.

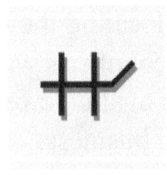

25 – THE SECOND DAY

Place of activity: Great Goddess Ma-l's domain
Date: year 1 of the Ma-lean calendar, G-day 2
Chronicler: Angel Bluefeather
Department of Warrior and Realm History

Something's happening, but I'm not sure what it is. Lovely Angel Vera has been absent since she left abruptly yesterday, while Liv and Lillian did not show up for duty this morning. I have also noticed that Angel Lev is working alone – Great Goddess Enola also left yesterday after a short meeting with Great One Amaterasu and Vac. Ma-l, Saka, and Olaf have been busy in the kitchen, covering for the missing help. Student Pau, Marshall, and Geir are taking care of shuttling food and dishes to and from the various stations, while keeping things tidy. The place is buzzing.

I notice two pairs of elders walking the grounds, whose energies are poorly aligned with the celebration. They act like strangers to each other, but I pick up a signal between them – they work as a team while it appears they are looking for someone or something. I ask Master Qo'ai-Marael, who's on one of her rare visits, if she can tell me anything about the four Masters.

"They are Angels Niamh and Tealsky – old acquaintances from way back – the others are Rashnu and Theyia. You may want to introduce yourself to make them feel welcome," she advises with a corner smile.

It sounds like brilliant advice – without the usual lovers around, I feel somewhat out of place myself.

I walk straight towards Niamh and Tealsky with the intention of politely offering my services. They look at me for a moment that betrays I am being fully evaluated, before they warm up to the proposition.

"What makes you think our privacy is in need of assistance, Angel Bluefeather," Tealsky asks, flirting with sarcasm.

"Perhaps it's the fact that you stick out of the crowd as the only Angels not sharing the joy – you, and another couple that brushed by me not too long ago."

"Does it affect your own sense of well-being to the extent you must investigate?" Niamh takes turn.

At this point I regret my move, but it's too late to back down.

"I have dealt with many a fresh arrival over the last few months – my help is available to those who wish to ease into their new environment – no strings attached."

"It is quite gallant of you, Angel," Tealsky says, "but what can you possibly tell us about the realms that differs from what has already been said?"

"It is true I cannot enlighten you on what this Oneness has not revealed yet, but perhaps the telling is not as important as the company."

"Alright then, walk with us and we'll see how it develops from there," Niamh surrenders.

We leave the noisy crowd as I take them to the creek trail. At first we say nothing, for it is the thing to do – then Tealsky stops abruptly and looks at me squarely.

"We are aware you are one of the chroniclers – I believe we know most of you, but not all – perhaps you can give us an update on who's who."

It's a tough proposition considering we were just given instructions by Le Lien to lock the team from inquiry. But I started this whole thing – diplomacy first.

"You mean to tell me that your old friend Qo'ai-Marael hasn't made the list available to you?"

"Friendships, as it turns out, do not last forever. So no, she hasn't, Angel."

I am almost convinced Master Tealsky deems me exploitable.

"Why don't we start with what you have then I will be most obliged to top the list?" I offer.

I sense a hesitation. I wish Angel Khaldun was around to read the nuances of our interaction.

This time, Niamh speaks.

"You turn the tables, Angel Bluefeather, are you not allowed to tell?"

"It is for those who wish to be known to show themselves, Master; I am not at liberty to divulge the identities of my co-workers, unless the nature of the enquiry entails a recommendation from one of them. If you wish to know, the department is the place to ask."

"OK, so tell us if I have this right: Grisha, Khaldun, Qo'ai-Marael, Gretchen, Monique, and you," she says

Something's not right because Angel Monique only made a brief appearance in Ma-l's realm with two villagers before returning to Xarn's on day -2 – too small a window for any elder to know of her and her work.

"Your sources run deep, Master Niamh, since Angel Monique operates in an off-limit realm – I have no idea how you got to know she's on the team," I say, somewhat puzzled.

"We have our ways," Tealsky asserts.

"Then our lists are identical," I lie.

At this point, I wish to end the conversation – they do as well. We decide to walk back and part at the entrance of the gathering grounds.

I need to speak with Vac or one of the Le Lien girls, but not until those four are off the realm. I hear, from the laughter in the kitchen, that Lillian has returned.

Good timing.

26 – CONFLICTING NUANCES

Zone of nuance: Great Goddess Ma-l's domain
Date: year 1 of the Ma-lean calendar, G-day 2
Chronicler: Angel Khaldun
Honorary member, Department of
Warrior and Realm History

My good friend Angel Bluefeather is walking away with two elder Masters. Based on my readings of their auratic fields, there are dissonances in their spectra. I have observed other Angels from the same group with similar emissions. If I were to pass judgment, I would say it is plausible these Masters are not here to enjoy themselves; rather, their reasons to partake in the celebration may not be to its benefit. Many discreet nuances indicate I am not the only guest to notice – Angel Qo'ai-Marael is also aware of the discordance.

The energy started shifting in the late morning of yesterday when Great One Amaterasu appeared for a brief meeting with Master Vac and Great Goddess Enola. Slightly beforehand, Angel Vera showed signs of agitation that could only have pertained to information she must have received via private channels. The tones between her energy field then, and those of the later meeting were closely matched. Interestingly, other nuances in the form of juxtaposed overtones also lined up with the aforementioned dissonance, meaning there is a possible relation between yesterday's events and the presence of these elder Masters in the reality of the realms.

While the gathering emanates harmony and joy to the benefit of the fundamental tone, anything that navigates against its current is proportionally highlighted. For those in my line of work, the culprits are akin to mini vortexes in a field of light.

A quick view from where I stand:

The front of the hostess' kitchen opens onto a cabana with the main buffet set to its left. The meadows spread beyond it for hundreds of yards, until they meet with the creek, and farther, the wooded area in the distance. Picnic tables are set as to not obstruct the view of the stages. One enters the patio to the gardens through a back door between the sink counter and the pantry. All the baking is done in the outdoor brick ovens located near the aromatic herb section.

Working with Geir and Marshall allows for the best vantage point, especially since the portals – decorated by Angel Lev to make them look like curtained doorways – are in plain view to the right of the cabana.

Master Grisha, who chronicles from the Great Hall, occasionally lets me know who's about to come through, but I don't hear from him often and traffic is incessant. On one of those rare occasions, the Angel informs me that Masters Jaco and Lo-shen are due to arrive. I ready myself during the roughly three minutes it takes for a crossing via Joonas Halls, for a solid evaluation of the visitors. Much has been rumored about Angel Jaco – he is reportedly disliked by those who inadvertently made contact with him.

As the curtains part, I am witness of the presence of two very powerful Masters. Their auratic signatures substantially veer off the main hue, but not necessarily disharmoniously. Oddly, they do not appear to belong here either. There is something ancient and immutable about the both of them – like laws onto themselves – qualities I also see in Masters such as Vac or Great One Amaterasu.

While I was told elder Jaco came from the first group of Angels, Lo-shen is well-known amongst historians for her role behind the consolidation of poorly organized tribal factions into the Guild. She is a much esteemed figure for her achievements, but also – and perhaps unfairly – reduced to living in the shadow of Guild mythology, for she is now mostly forgotten as the result of a millennia-long leave of absence. The same could be said of Master Jaco who moved onto lengthy and distant assignments after the Great Battles.

I am not at liberty to assume their presence is other than recreational, or that they are here on matters unrelated to the christening of the realms, but the nuances don't lie – they are neither integral nor separate from the celebration. I can only stipulate that their attendance is of significance on multiple levels.

Interestingly enough, they proceed in my direction.

"Greetings, Angel Khaldun!" Master Lo-shen forwards, as the two reach the food counter. "There is no need between us to pretend that we did not expect crossing paths."

"I was indeed informed of your visit; though, I am unaware it was to connect with me."

"Well, yes and no," Master Jaco adds; "your skills precede you, Angel; thus, we seek their services. You are not yet to demand why, but just know it is highly desirable from our standpoint, that this event be recorded by a group of chroniclers who just happen to have the best inter-realm view of it. If it is agreeable with you, feel free to share the contents of your findings in the field of nuances, around the movements of certain groups of elders."

"It is rare that I share so freely," I say, "but from my work as a historian, your respective achievements precede you as well; therefore I consider it my duty to honor your request to a point."

I tell what I know – within set group guidelines – about my encounters with the "mini vortexes," also, I suggest they meet with Angel Bluefeather who has recently left with the two elders. I intentionally omit the part about Angel Vera and the meeting between Vac, Amaterasu, and Warrior Enola – too much privacy at stakes.

"Thank you, Angel," Master Lo-shen says, smiling. "We already know about the other stuff you feel rightfully reluctant to share."

They leave with a polite nod. I feel somewhat dazzled by the fact they could read me so easily, just from imperceptible nuances. I did say "powerful Masters" though.

I get back to the tasks. Angel Lillian has returned with Geir to join me at dishes.

I see Bluefeather approach the cabana alone, as Masters Jaco and Lo-shen leave it. I make eye contact with him – he appears puzzled – but then, he walks back in the direction of the creek, flanked by his two interceptors.

27 – A PUZZLING REPORT

Area of activity: Le Lien Headquarters
Date: year 1 of the Realms, G-day 2
Chronicler: Angel Spencer, team Le Lien

Vera just returned from her inspection of the tunnels with Goddess Enola – the contents of her report are extremely dire. The presence of seed algorithms planted in the lanes irrevocably incriminates Caax and Dzalarhons. Guild Headquarters – back in the original Oneness – must be informed at once. It is beyond an act of treason, it is one of offensive – an attack. Though we still lack peremptory proof the trespassers are responsible for it, early results from the reversed analysis of foreseeable scenarios point to a match. From an intuitive standpoint, they are already guilty. I must notify Portals and Qwave of the incident under the code of secrecy, for the gathering must go on at all cost, unimpeded. Their techs will be requiring assistance from the three Warriors to access the tunnels of the aborted realms, so that the seeds can be neutralized. I ask Vera to contact Enola immediately to seek her collaboration. I shall wait on Ma-l and Xarn for just the right time window – as much as I wish to not involve them, I don't see a way around it.

The meeting is in a few hours. After Vera's confession of her suspicions of Lo-shen being *Third Eye*, I am beginning to think we may already have Guild involvement in the case. As to Jaco, I have no clue – he was against the Great Ones' choice of saving humanity, but he wasn't siding with Joonas either. I am told he admired the Dove for his mettle, not his madness.

The act of reseeding the old tunnels is without a doubt meant to destabilize the new system, with the intention of incapacitating it, while George's fundamental makeup – corruption et al – gets reinstated, effectively shutting the realms from each other and aborting the expansion of the new universe. It is essentially a deed of malfeasance against the wish of the original One – something up Joonas's alley with Hektor – but we know for a fact at Le Lien, that he has zero part in it. He chose to remain in the old tunnels to relive the fate of the Warriors – by immersing himself in the solitude of the stone until he comes out of it purified.

No, it appears someone doesn't want him to find that peace, or wishes to inculpate him, since he was the original seed coder. Also, that someone would have to be aware of the corruption that saw to George's emergence, in order to exploit it – we have categorical knowledge it couldn't be Joonas. That leaves us with anyone from the original team, or the group of Angels in charge of placing the Warriors' spirits in the stone – precisely someone who didn't want to see the realms succeed.

Angel Vac informs me he wishes to connect. I let him in.

"Spencer," he says, "I believe we must pool our resources around what is being played in the background of the ceremony. We don't have much time until tonight's meeting and not enough data either, to gain the upper hand over the situation – unless Le Lien has something new. Amaterasu and I have been made aware Jaco and Lo-shen still operate under *Third Eye*. The organization went in sleep mode – or rather, feigned its own demise – to concentrate on the case that is about to deploy in this reality. They are undercover Guild officials and we must immediately engage in a working relationship with them if we want to see proper legal proceedings regarding our detainees. It is my understanding that Caax and Dzalarhons – as well as a number of other Masters – deem they are under no defined jurisdiction; thus, not chargeable with any wrongdoings, as well as immune to investigative enquiry. Considering we don't have a judicial system to speak of, or any form of punitive means beyond holding someone in a force field for a day, they may be right."

Vac waits for my turn to speak.

"I'm glad we have help from the Guild," I say. "The news that came to me is the worst I have received since Joonas threatened an invasion – we're talking newly planted seed algorithms ready to morph into a new version of George."

Vac pauses as if to plan his next move.

"I must return to Amaterasu without further delay. I trust you understand the depths of these matters – please be prepared with a case that leaves no doubt as to the intentions behind these acts of sabotage. Our elders' wisdom favors caution over fast-acting; therefore we can't afford to be bogged down by a lack of clarity. One more thing: keep Ma-1 and Xarn out of it – the foreseeable outcomes are not worth the risk. Amaterasu will connect with Enola, Qwave, and Portals – Angel Vera may work with them if she wishes."

Vac leaves through his carry-on portal.

It's been a long day but it feels like it's just about to begin – I must now prepare for the emergency meeting.

28 – THE MEETING

Place of activity: The New Guild Center
Date: year 1 of the Realms, G-day 2
Chronicler: Senior Master Qo'ai-Marael,
Honorary member Department of
Warrior and Realm History

We are still waiting for Great One Amaterasu and Angel Vac. Six elders from the New Guild Center have been selected as representatives of the Assembly via a system of lottery. All were available.

The list:

- Master Paca: New Guild Affairs
- Master Lars: Communications
- Master Honoré: Student Training
- Master Tet: Branch Coordination
- Master Farai: Portals
- Master Mudiwa: Guild History

Masters Jaco and Lo-shen have joined us on the Great One's recommendation.

I shall assume the role of coordinator while Angel Spencer from Le Lien, will present the case. Great One Amaterasu is to preside over the meeting – Master Vac will mediate.

The last two arrive – all are seated.

After a round of introductions, Amaterasu explains the reasons for the meeting, the role of each participant, and what is being asked of them, at which point Masters Jaco and Lo-shen's identities are revealed. I am more surprised by the news that *Third Eye* is still operative than by knowing the two are Guild agents.

Angel Spencer is then called to present the case.

He is surgical and keeps his passions in check. The enumeration of complaints leads quickly to the description of the horrid act of malfeasance – murmurs are being heard from the panel of elders. Master Spencer then closes his report, stressing on the importance of acting swiftly. Le Lien's recommendation is to turn the detainees over to *Third Eye* before they are allowed back in the realms.

Amaterasu asks the two Guild representatives to come forward in order to bring light on the nature of their investigation, and how it leads to Caax and Dzalarhons' incrimination for acts against the two Onenesses.

Master Jaco:

"Dzalarhons is no stranger to most of us – she was on the original team with Masters Vac, Qo'ai-Marael, and Farai, a group to which I also belonged. She was one of the original coders with Joonas. When Guild discontentment arose at the time of the Battles, she showed no interest in siding with Hektor for reasons similar to mine. We both chose distant assignments with the intention of finding healing space. We considered the choice of the Ones to be ill-fated."

"At the time, Master Lo-shen and I were agents of *Third Eye*. We created a list of all the Angels who voiced their opposition to that choice – I deemed it my duty to put my own name on it. The purpose was to keep an eye on potential defectors to Hektor, as well as moles inside the Guild – history is nearly non-existent in that regard. Oddly, we were responsible for forcing hundreds of suspected spies into joining the rogue league, or face 'consciousness freeze,' as we called it – I doubt you will find mention of it anywhere. But there was a group that stood against the choice of the Ones, and which also opposed Joonas's heavy-fisted approach; thus, we created a list for them as well. Caax and Dzalarhons were on it, so were a number of elders from the latest arrival – namely: Niamh, Rashnu, Tealsky, and Theyia, plus a dozen or so of their followers."

Master Lo-shen:

"Master Jaco and I founded *Third Eye* around the time of the consolidation of the tribes of Angels into the Guild – essentially as a means to filter out the most unruly components at the base to these groups' divisional reality. One may say *Third Eye* was more of an assignment than it was an organization intimately tied to the core of the Guild – we later took it with us to our corner of the universal Oneness. Le Lien was soon created, by no other than Master Vac, to replace it – though the founder has strictly remained on the outside as a consultant."

"Vac first informed me of an irregularity among those who chose distant assignments on the premise of their dissatisfaction with the Guild's decision – they were all observed in the same area on a random basis, for the purpose of meeting secretly. Based on retroactive, early portal scanning methods, their gatherings were frequent. Predictably, they used a system of relays through a series of little-used routes to access their meeting grounds. The discovery was accidental – one of their portals failed during a dare by a denizen of the underworld, or Interverse, and had to be serviced. Spatial memory revealed unusual activity that led to its connectedness to all relay points. It was a meticulously constructed web that highlighted a strong desire to hide. *Third Eye* was reactivated."

Master Jaco:

"We were in a desirable position to infiltrate their meetings. I had voiced my opposition to the deal with the Ones, and with Master Lo-shen, we – for all to see – shut *Third Eye* down; an act that added exponential value to our credibility as rebels. We arranged to 'accidentally' connect, as the result of which we were overwhelmingly welcomed into the group. Its name is 'Seventeen' or the Roman 'XVII,' as in the number of attendants at its first gathering."

Master Lo-shen:

"Unlike Hektor which gained enormous traction, XVII was slow to coalesce, in spite of Dzalarhons and Caax's shared vision of competing with Joonas's group. It was obvious there was great discomfort around the lopsidedness of their weak standing, but they chose to hide while Hektor thrived in full view. One may say there was a dishonest approach to their emergence, by choosing to exist in the shadows of both the Guild and Hektor, and it's probably why the group remained atrophied. Nonetheless, their motives were far from diminutive. With time, they came to silently despise both organizations. But it wasn't until they began to increasingly immerse themselves in the search for auspicious probabilities to the development of the realms that flags were raised for *Third Eye*; so, we started recruiting members to keep tags on all of XVII's moves."

Master Jaco:

"After Vac and young Master Olaf crossed into Warrior Ma-1's realm, and the way to the Great Hall of Angel City was found, two of XVII's members – Masters Jen and Lawrence – volunteered at Portals to be among the firsts to explore the complex maze of tunnels that refused access to the realms. They commuted regularly back to the secret meeting grounds to report of their findings. Dzalarhons claimed she had found what had caused the shut off of the realms. She attributed the mishap to an inadvertent programming error of her own doing, and prided herself in the irony of it – the Warrior collective would fail without a battle. But her glee was short-lived; instead of being dismantled by the Guild, Hektor was given a new lease on existence, while the Dove saved the realms by retrieving the virgin codes that activated the new tunnels and brought life into Joonas Halls."

Master Lo-shen:

"In the meantime, Jen and Lawrence – who had witnessed first-hand the work of Snake, Portals, and Qwave – ended up locked inside Angel City following the collapse of the mother reality. As soon as the lane between Amaterasu and Saka's stones became active, XVII swiftly enlisted into the last group of volunteers, armed with live seed algorithms, with the aim of disabling the entire system of access and communication between the New Center and each of the realms. Furthermore, Dzalarhons had another plan – she saw the connective forces that held Joonas Halls to the realms of Hektor, and thus modified the algorithms so that they would mutate into a vortex that would neutralize the stones, simultaneously bringing forth the collapse of the realms and the world of Hektor. As the result of having infiltrated their meetings and been made aware of their plans, it is clear to *Third Eye* that XVII means to inflict irreversible ruin to both Onenesses. This concludes our report."

The two Masters return to their seats. Great One Amaterasu comes forward to ask the members of the panel if they have any questions.

Master Tet rises.

"What assurance do we have you are who you say you are, and this meeting is not just smoke and mirrors?"

Jaco answers.

"There are two ways to look at it, Master Tet, either the detainees are the villains or we are. One way or the other, you have a situation. I believe you are exercising due caution; I would not do otherwise in your place."

Amaterasu thanks Master Tet. She then speaks.

"Masters Jaco and Lo-shen have my full trust. Angel Vac and I have remained in communication with *Third Eye* – all of their reports have now been made available to Le Lien. Up to this point and in spite of what we knew, XVII only posed a hypothetical threat, but it appears we misjudged the group's reach and determination."

Master Paca stands.

"We have no jurisdiction over Guild affairs and no judicial system of our own – no foreseeable scenario prepared us for this dramatic turn of events. Even if we agreed to hand over the two detainees to Guild agents, on what grounds are we to deport the entire XVII back to the league of Masters?"

Vac answers.

"This is why we are meeting. This panel is empowered to pass emergency laws – we have six elders, one security official, a Great One presiding, coordinators and mediators. The case has been presented, and the risk assessment made clear – we are in the presence of a class 5 security breach with massive implications to all of existence. Master Qo'ai-Marael, please state your proposition."

It is my turn to speak – I read from my notes:

"In the light of the New Guild Center's decision to forgo institutional executive power, its residents are deemed fully capable of self-policing, and thus entrusted and empowered to act – within the natural guidelines of common sense and reason – towards the safety of the whole at the risk of no individual. In the event threats are immediate and covered under defined jurisdictions, all elements pertinent to aforementioned threats will be handed over to the legitimate authority. This law covers realm cases forwarded by their representatives to the New Guild Center."

"I propose we pass this law under emergency protocol, with the provision of revising and amending it after its expiry date, 6 realm months and one day from enactment," I conclude.

I suddenly feel extremely exhausted.

29 – THE MEETING II

Area of activity: New Guild Center Headquarters
Date: year 1 of the Realms, G-day 2
Chronicler: Angel Spencer, team Le Lien

Master Qo'ai-Marael brings forth the first security law drafted by the New Guild Center. It gets voted three to two with one abstention. As per Guild rule under which this meeting operates, and until further laws pertinent to the workings of the center in regard to the realms are enacted, consensus is not applicable under critical emergency. Masters Dzalarhons and Caax are due for immediate deportation to main Guild Headquarters to stand trial. Amaterasu and Vac will accompany Master Jaco and the restrained criminals to Keyhole Lake, where Guild security will take over.

Le Lien will round up Rashnu, Niamh, Theyia, Jen, Tealsky, and Lawrence for a series of interrogations. They are suspected of having planted corrupt seeds in Ma-1 and Xarn's tunnels. They are unaware of Jaco and Lo-shen's statuses; hence, the agents' identities will not be revealed until all suspects are either arrested or cleared. The XVII members will not be able to lie, but they will be under the assumption they are untouchable. After all the names, which we already obtained from Lo-shen, are cross-referenced with the collected testimonies, the entire corrupt organization will be deported.

All agenda items have been addressed and all parties have spoken. Amaterasu closes the meeting.

We all look exhausted, and save for the panel which is still in the throes of external debate, all of us are relieved. The abstention vote came from Master Lars who demanded that a witness be present. It was explained to him that the nature of the meeting forbade witnesses not bound to the rule of secrecy from testifying. I proposed, under the clause of exception, to fetch Great Goddess Enola, Angel Gretchen, and agent Vera, but the rest of the panel didn't see the point of it and voted against it.

Gathering day number two will be remembered across the ages by those of us who work in the background – I promise myself to get out of the office to join the celebration before it is over.

30 – A CASE OF ODD BEHAVIOR

Place of action: the Great Hall
Date: year 1 of the Realms, G-day 3
Chronicler: Angel Grisha
Department of Warrior and Realm History

I witness erratic movement on the main floor of the Great Hall. Most of the elders normally present at the cafeteria are missing, at the exception of Master Emile and a group of his jovial followers. I was actually hoping to connect with Master Lo-shen, who had asked for details on realm history. Angel Tet informs me that she came in very early to pick up a coffee to go then left in a hurry.

I cannot help notice that the tunnel entrances to the three realms – as well as all those on the ground floor to the developmentally arrested worlds – are kept under tight surveillance by Angels pretending to have matters to take care of nearby. The portals to Xarn and Enola's domains from the main floor via Joonas Halls are also under surveillance – but most Angels wouldn't know. That's why they had me work the Kremlin back in the day – I can smell intrigue from a galaxy away.

Vac stops by briefly.

"Document all you can, Grisha – it will serve history well," he says.

It's all I need to hear to get things flowing.

Aside from informing Khaldun of the approach of

venerable visitors such as the Masters from the original team, or the occasional Great One capable of assuming the flesh like Amaterasu, I survey the stone tunnels. Everyone knows I'm one of the chroniclers, so my movements are of no consequence to anyone. I see Master Lawrence of Portals at thirty-three, stairwell three. He doesn't see me. He enters the tunnel to be immediately followed by the guard on duty who, a second ago, acted as one of the floor's resting tenants – I wait. A half hour passes. Suddenly, the undercover Angel comes out running, then vanishes through a portal – Lawrence is nowhere in sight.

I know there's no exit out of Ma-l's tunnel, so the Master still has to be in there. It's not a very long corridor either – I wait some more. After a while, it is clear the Angel has followed a different route. It is most perplexing since it implies an intrinsic knowledge of the lanes not available to Guild Masters. I now understand the guard's reaction.

I try to connect with Angel Khaldun but to no avail. Surprisingly, the line has been disconnected. Instead Master Lo-shen materializes by my side.

"It's best to keep this between you and Spencer at Le Lien. I assume it is agreeable with you, Angel Grisha – consider yourself on a new assignment. You can go on with chronicling as a cover, but you are now to report strictly to security, to which you are granted direct access. I understand this may be too much to ask of you, but I need your word on this," she says.

I am slow to respond. On what authority is she asking me to spy?

"What are you?" I ask hesitantly.

"I'm *Third Eye*, a lot like the old KGB – obsolete, but far more efficient and discriminating," she claims.

Angel Spencer appears through the same portal used by the elder.

"Master Lo-shen has my full support," he says. "Are you willing to take on the oath of secrecy for the remaining of the celebration and possibly beyond, or do I have to remove you from your post and make sure that what you know doesn't spread around? If we didn't think you were qualified, we wouldn't have allowed you to come this far."

I prefer a less conditional approach, but I accept with assured enthusiasm – I have been missing the action, so I am delighted by the fact the realms can provide the occasional mission.

"I assume you know what just happened in there," he says. "I am assigning agent Liv to the case – you and she will work together on both sides of the gates – you're in charge of the Great Hall. Angel Vera will also be reporting from inside the tunnels – we want to make sure that whoever enters, comes out."

Lo-shen and Spencer leave the way they came. I connect with Angel Liv – our line is live.

"Welcome to Le Lien, agent Grisha," she confirms.

31 – THE TUNNEL SEARCH

Places of action: the tunnels
Date: year 1 of the realms, G-day 4
Chronicler: Angel Vera, team Le Lien,
Guild archivist

What a day yesterday was! Though Le Lien managed to round up a number of XVII members, while Jaco took Dzalarhons and Caax back to original Guild Headquarters, we lost Niamh, Theyia, Rashnu, Tealsky, Lawrence, and Jen to the tunnels. Lo-shen informed us earlier of the sophisticated knowledge XVII had of the old réseau, but we are taken aback by the latest feat. We conclude they have created a link between the new and the old system, possibly by tapping data out of the ghost memory of the deleted gestalt, with the use of the seed algorithms – the same way we accessed Angel City from the Guild, on the image of the collapsed mother reality.

I also met with Vac, Amaterasu, and Spencer to go over the details of my assignment, at which time Vac was informed Angel Grisha had just joined the force – a move he and I highly approve of.

Vac is accompanied by Sam the dog, as the three of us enter Ma-l's tunnel – the hunt is on for the missing rogue Angels.

I hear the conversation between the two canids. I thought from the get-go there was something odd about

Sam – well, there is. He's like the idiot savant of dogs – all intuition, full blissed-out trust. If Angels kept pets, he would be the perfect model – an eternal subject of awe and endearment.

Lawrence is the only Angel who was seen entering the tunnels – Le Lien is scanning signatures for the others. We are where it is estimated he escaped.

"Sir Vac," I hear Sam say, "I smell a presence where I stand, but with another step, it's gone. I think we should proceed straight through this wall."

Then he's gone.

Vac holds to the lead as we cross.

Wow, just like that – this guy should be made an honorary Guild Master!

It's not totally dark in here – the surface of the walls emits a faint green glow that makes for an eerie monochromatic environment. Sure enough, I locate an embedded seed. Qwave provided a scanner that doubles as a latch-on modifier – essentially, it freezes the growth of the seed without killing it. Full deletion could potentially trap us on the wrong side of the link.

I have shared this with Liv, Spencer, and Lillian – my take is that Jen and Lawrence knew a lot more about the system of tunnels than the rest of Portals; thus, I have no doubt they tweaked their findings to stifle the work of their department. It has me thinking they might even have struck a deal with George. I understand it sounds far-fetched and I could be wrong, but I have been known to be spot-on with crazier ideas.

That theory puts XVII substantially ahead of Portals in its knowledge of maneuvering around the old lanes – especially with Dzalarhons' work with the original team, and her coding skills at their disposal. Angels Axel and Ilia excused themselves from the festivities to return to the drawing board. It is expected that with new data input and Qwave's assistance, they will be able to catch up and follow in our footsteps. For now, Sam's the savior.

A series of twist and turns brings us to the open light – right above Ma-1's valley, out of Snake's collapsed tunnel. I inform Liv who's down there with Lillian – the info gets forwarded to Le Lien central then onto Jaco, Lo-shen, and Amaterasu. Everyone who's on the assignment adjusts their end as they receive updates. As the team builds the case in real time, a singular consciousness emerges with the purpose of locating and harnessing the specifics of resolution – on a good day it's like perfect clockwork.

We return to the darkness – this time, Sam leads us to the link that connects with the corridor to old Angel City. We arrive at the carbon copy of the entryway we took to get into Ma-1's tunnel, at thirty-three and three. My head spins from the convolutions of the near endless possibilities present. More seeds are found and frozen. The Great Hall is barely lit, but any light is a sign of activation of the lanes – the XVII team is hard at work letting its self-locating programs run loose all over the maze.

We are getting news that Axel and Ilia have been able to isolate our first link and have crossed. More of Portals and Qwave are preparing for a massive mapping party of all the connecting points between the old and the new. Luckily for all, there are only three open realms, and the corridors to the abandoned caves are the only ones with enough strength to carry the links for now. It doesn't mean it will stay that way forever. The seed algorithms grow the second they latch on the image of the demised gestalt – the thing is that we have to stop them before they start communicating with each other, and coalescing into a whole that will permanently shut all tunnels.

Vac and I agree; some of the rogue Masters are somewhere in the ghost City. As a matter of fact, Sam who had been silent for a while, is heard saying:

"Sir Vac, there is foraging down below. By the sound of it, I'd say someone walked straight into a hornet's nest."

Sam doesn't seem to care much for the basic laws of physics – he leads us down thirty-seven floors directly under the main hall where the entrances to the failed realms are located – all without the use of the stairs or portals – brilliant. He enters the tunnel into Snake's world where the noise is being heard – we follow. We come to a sight Dzalarhons could not have foreseen.

As it turns out, a seed inadvertently latched onto Snake's fire, while a hail of sparks is seen surrounding and harassing Angel Lawrence – a hornet's nest, hey? Oh, Sam, where are you from?

As if my mind wasn't already tested enough, Amaterasu appears out of nowhere to gird the XVII member in a magnetic jacket.

Snake's voice rises.

"This one didn't look legitimate, Great One. I understand these tunnels well since I carved them, so I know who's supposed to be left inside them and who's not. This Angel is trying to awaken the one that is to never return; I can tell his purpose is dark. Others are roaming in the adjacent lanes, permit me to stop them."

"Do as you must, Snake," Amaterasu replies.

She turns to us.

"Nice job, team, I'm taking this one with me."

She and Lawrence are gone.

32 – THE FINAL TALLY

Area of activity: New Guild Center Headquarters
Date: year 1 of the Realms, G-day 4
Chronicler: Angel Spencer, team Le Lien

The question of the XVII members' origin arose. Lo-shen explained that though many of the Angels that could not be accepted into the Guild went on to rule the underworld – layers of existence that rarely interact with "surface realities" – many managed to slip through the cracks. Dzalarhons paid notice. As to that underworld, it is by virtue of its complex makeup, a universe of its own that is said to counterbalance the energy of the whole – officially, it goes by the name of Interverse.

Unlike Hektor which was formed by Masters, the original XVII was made of tribal leaders who had successfully entered the Guild in spite of their aversion to the consolidation of the various families. *Third Eye* eventually became aware of the infiltration, but as loose elements, these Angels didn't seem to pose a problem at the time – a least not until the age of the Battles. They apparently needed a trigger, and the conflict that birthed Hektor was also what spurred XVII into coalescing.

It is difficult to map the psychology of a fallen Angel. Let me just say that Dzalarhons was born of the same fiber that made Joonas – extremely powerful beings with a grudge towards a humanity that had imprinted its stigmas onto their souls at a very early stage of their developments. According to both Vac and Jaco, Dzalarhons was always forceful, bordering on arrogant, but she was extremely capable in many areas that were short on Angels, plus she wasn't afraid to put herself in the path of danger to see to the end of an assignment. In perspective, they both admit she should have been among the firsts to be filtered out of the Guild, and sent on her way to shape the Interverse.

Jaco is just reporting that she, Caax, and Lawrence are now in a state of suspension following compounded evidence of breach of Guild protocol.

It is my opinion that their methods are consistent with the work of fanatical fringe groups, as seen among humans. Their actions are meant to yield results of apocalyptic proportions – to them, arrests and trials are heroic markers along the pursuit of causes. XVII wanted nothing less than to see the Guild, Hektor, the realms, and humanity cave in as one.

Le Lien has assembled fifty-nine elders for questioning – all of them who, at one point or another, were associated with Dzalarhons and XVII. It is likely most of them will be returned to Guild Headquarters under Jaco and Lo-shen's watchful eye, for further inquiry.

Many of the seed algorithms have been found and put into freeze mode by Portals and Qwave techs. The fact the links are being saved, is a quantum leap for the two departments which had already put Angel City behind them as part of archeological reality. Of course, the sanctity of the old tunnels is to be preserved – the management of the lanes is the responsibility of the Warriors as a collective.

What Angel Jen and Lawrence were able to do that Portals couldn't, was to interlink the individual tunnels to the realms – the whole hundred and forty-eight of the combined presumed-active and arrested ones – in a way that allowed them to exit through whichever lane they wished, from any entry point. Not a great achievement considering they could only return to the Great Hall or the three open realms – it was nonetheless a major improvement over the maddening randomness others had to live with, and a great asset while maneuvering within Angel City. It goes without saying that if the realms had been open before George's demise, Jen, Lawrence, and XVII would have been in possession of the master key – something only the Warriors could own by right.

It is being hypothesized that the two renegade Masters had seen through gestalt George's weaknesses and made a deal with it – but the force that had handed over the key was also the one that – figuratively speaking – had changed the locks.

The remaining of the roaming elders has been located – it's just a matter of time before we get to them. They managed to sneak out of Snake's reach into an area too sensitive for the might of his great fire. The seeds are gathering strength at a far more rapid rate than anticipated, for there is now enough energy in the tunnels out of Angel City for linkage – with Jen and enough seeds loose in the réseau, much damage is foreseen.

Qwave and Portals are on the line.

33 – CHASE THROUGH THE MAZE

Places of action: the tunnels
Date: year 1 of the realms, G-day 4
Chronicler: Angel Vera, team Le Lien,
Guild archivist

Time has its own beat in the tunnels – mostly that hours fly by. Amaterasu informs us that we are in the fourth day of the celebration and that the gathering is peaking.

"Ma-1 is sensing something's amiss but she must hold the fort," the Great One shares.

Nonetheless, the XVII roamers have escaped through new links, deep into the lanes of the Warriors, while Snake can no longer help. The techs from Qwave have been able to home on some of the seeds, stabilize them into fixed-mode and clock them down – so there's a chance that there may not be enough of them to gel into a gestalt of significant strength. It's all contingent on the technology, and whether they are capable of self-cloning or not. Qwave is not seeing any potential for it, which is all I need to know at the present.

Not everything is fine and dandy for the loose cannons in the tunnels, because their seeds give away the links, which allows for us to find more of both. As the game goes, eventually someone is going to run out of chips. Their knowledge of the corridors is as finite as what the maze is willing to surrender – my intuitions tell me their backs are about to meet the end wall.

When seeds are not present to point to the links, Sam finds the paths – they're all game to wonderdog. He lets Vac know it's as much fun as chasing squirrels, which as the story goes, is also how he finds himself crossing into impossible dimensions – generally, where squirrels aren't found.

Well, it's when it gets interesting, because we land in a tavern-like grotto where a dozen drunken men are demanding a drink for their female buddy, who as it turns out, has just unwittingly stumbled upon them.

"A quaff fer th'laydee, bartenda!" one demands.

The cave is dim and there's no bartender as far as I can tell. Angel Jen – who's quite slender – is squeezed in between two burly sweaty humans with terrible manners.

The lot notices us.

"Hey, we got company – bring on the drinks!" one shouts. "Where's fuckin' Joonas!?"

The same question echoes twelve times.

Like clockwork, Amaterasu arrives to wrap the XVII member and her seeds in the latest fashion in straight jackets.

More shouts about women, drinks, and Joonas follow. The lights and the noise go out as we exit.

"What the hell was that all about?" I ask, my thoughts spiraling.

"It appears we found Joonas's lost team," Amaterasu says. "I shall explain one day. In the meantime, another good catch – congratulations!"

She leaves with doe-eyed Jen.

"Are you up for four more," Vac enquires.

"With you and Sam in the same room, how much more fun can a girl ask for?" I answer.

"Sir Vac, I'm not sure what the human female is saying, but it's making my head tilt to the right," Sam remarks.

I keep a mounting chuckle under control.

"It's perhaps because she's not human," Vac adds.

Sam sits on it for a sec.

"Makes sense," he says, as his thoughts wander to a place only Sam knows.

Angel Jen was easy – she simply ran out of steam. The bar scene didn't help. I could almost feel bad for her if it wasn't for the fact she chose to play a very naughty game. I wonder what tipped her boat for her to wind up at the foot of a miserable upslope. We probably will never know.

Four more, Vac says – but last I heard, they worked in pairs. Sam is not feeling the squirrel element in the present equation.

"Sir Vac, the ones we're looking for have stopped moving; I'm not so good when that happens," he says.

"Your food bowl doesn't move either, yet you always find it, even when it's hidden," Vac returns with humor.

"I reckon," Sam says.

With that, we move out of the maze, back into the Great Hall of Angel City. Somehow, and in spite of the neutralized seeds, the place appears brighter – not good.

The lighting at the far end of the floor indicates that someone is still in there, either hiding or looking for a way out – or some other thing. But when we get to it, all we find are empty rooms. The glow is still here but it has merged with the one that has been following us since we got in. The Great Hall's lighting – as the first Angels to reach the place recall – was meant to guide them through their first steps. As more came, the brightness increased proportionally. So what is it we're supposed to find? Sam is ahead of us sniffing his way in and out of old offices, stores, and food places, zigzagging and circling as if chasing a roaming miniature vortex.

"Do you mind sharing?" Vac asks.

"Give me a moment, Sir," Sam replies.

Vac turns to me.

"With our combined skills, I trust we could easily locate and subdue these errant Angels, but we both intuitively agree that it is what is expected of us. Am I reading this accurately?"

I nod and ask him to continue.

"We both sense there is a trap, but perhaps our friend here is not factored in. When Amaterasu briefed me, she advised me to proceed cautiously, with only the use of basic tools for minimal impact. Snake backed off on similar intuition. I observe you are able to lock on that frequency as well – that is indeed a gift, Vera."

I'm not quite sure where he's getting at, but I'm fine with the compliment. It's clear to me that there is foul play in the making – it has been too easy so far, considering what's at stake. I smell a setup. Vac is right – Sam is disrupting their plans. I am of the belief that because we're doing all we can to not jeopardize the gathering, caution is working against their projected outcome – things are not moving as fast as anticipated. I am beginning to see that their seeds need focused Angel energy in order to quickly reach maturity – the more the better – and that's why they are exposing themselves to lead us on a chase.

I share my views with Vac – he agrees.

I connect with Grisha to check where he's at. He informs me that he feels he's being taken for a ride, that somehow the four elders are able to go in and out at wish, without so much as caring for the frustrated guards. I tell him to not get involved and to take a step back.

"Pretend you're working in Moscow again," I say.

Spencer is on it as well. Everyone is now backing off and working in "human mode" – a slow, imprecise and error-prone way of doing things, but one that is bound to relax the pace. Sure enough, there is an imperceptible downgrading of visibility in the Great Hall.

As Vac and I wax logistical, Sam makes a great leap backwards to make room for an imposing figure; one that stands a few feet away looking at us like a bear who's been jarred out of hibernation.

"I didn't expect to see you so soon," Vac says, "but I admit this is somewhat out of our control."

"Since when has anything been out of your control?" the guttural voice returns.

"This one may surprise you – someone has changed the design of your seed programs and planted them all over the old tunnels," Vac says.

I interrupt.

"I don't believe we've been introduced."

"Joonas or the Dove, whichever of the two suits the particulars of the myth that precedes me," the apparition returns.

I freeze. I should have known. After all, we came very close to each other while he was roaming Eureka – particularly when he almost did Marshall and Jarred in. But me being Vera, my mind does not let me idle for more than a few seconds at a time.

"A myth would have been sweet, but it turns out I was part of doing damage control after you visited the neighborhood," I voice.

"You may refresh my memory on some of my misdeeds at the appropriate time, for now I believe you and I are on the same side of the present situation," he replies with pointed logic.

Vac and I update him on the case. He insists we keep a lid on his presence – at least for now. He's aware of XVII and tells us that Hektor had also kept a tab on them since the Battles – he's visibly not fond of Caax and Dzalarhons.

"From your explanation, the programs are modified to automatically latch on the ghost image of that detestable gestalt, while they feed on the energy of the tumult created by the search. I see that Dzalarhons capitalized on her mistakes rather than admitting she erred – typical," he says.

Joonas asks that we take him to the location of one the seeds in the tunnels. I tell Spencer to keep Portals and Qwave out of the way until further notice – he's reluctant, but he's in the office – field operation takes precedence.

On first inspection, the Hektor founder explains that the programs can only be momentarily stabilized before self-healing undoes the freeze and finds a way around further tampering – they can't be stopped. Oh joy! It turns out Qwave is wrong – the seeds can indeed self-clone, as well as make themselves undetectable by relocating the links, until whoever is left outside the system is forever prevented from entering the realms – meaning the entire New Guild Center. Joonas is clear – this is the job for an insider.

"George's ghost image must be destroyed – without anything to latch on, the programs are useless. Any other method will either be time-consuming – as far as I know you have two days at best before the seeds connect with each other – or if you manage to kill the image yourself, your teams will be locked in with no recourse. You must too understand that these programs will evolve one way or the other – if at a slower pace – without Angel raw vitality. There is much stored energy to tap from in the deep strata of this rocky formation," he says.

Joonas proposes that since his team is still around, he and they can operate from the inside, effectively shutting off the old lanes and Angel City from intruders, once and for all.

"I have matters to settle with that gestalt; a ghost image is more life that it deserves. One day, I may decide to come out – I will know then how to activate the seeds in a way that will not jeopardize the realms. Please, you must leave immediately – you don't even have the option of a choice. If Amaterasu has enough trust in me to name a hub after my person, know that I can be worthy of it. On a final note – without your friend here, you would be facing a very different outcome. We shall meet again!"

Of course, he meant Sam.

Joonas is now gone. I inform Spencer that we are pulling out. He assures me that all personnel are now out of the old maze. He has no idea where Niamh, Theyia, Tealsky, and Rashnu are – Le Lien has lost its tag on them. As far as I know, they can stay in Angel City where they belong – frozen in that one last motion – as stone figures in the center of its main floor.

34 – JEOPARDIZED PORTALS

Location: Great God Xarn's domain
Date: year 1 of Xarnean calendar, G-day 5
Chronicler: Angel Monique, genetics
Department of Warrior and Realm History

The celebration is in full swing. For the last three days, I have had the privilege to escort Skatu, Alice, and Jessie, who have been carrying supplies into Ma-l's realm. Wolf and I have become best friends. He tells me of his plans to work with Angel Lev and Great Goddess Enola on populating her domain – of course, details need to be further discussed. He is an endearing character. Great God Xarn is the most charming of hosts; he has made of my time in his world quite the delightful experience. It is beyond extraordinary what he has created here; I am particularly honoured to have been chosen to chronicle from his home.

Saka is around when she finds time away from her work at Ma-l's kitchen. Xarn rarely leaves the realm – when he does, he asks for an entire tribe to keep Wolf company by the tunnel's entrance. He did not take the Angel's intrusion well.

I have to admit that most of my report went on to study the inhabitants of the villages, so I am guilty of failing the history department. On the other hand, science has all to gain. Xarn has accepted my request to hold the post of appointed Angel to his realm, on the condition that I spend more time enjoying my surroundings and its people than analyzing them. I may have to endure the pleasure.

Jessie and Alice have taken me to a number of villages down river – one day, I hope to make it all the way to the ocean. The genetic diversity of their inhabitants is closely matched by the flora that surrounds them. I forever find myself at the center of a kaleidoscope of never-ending wonderment.

We come to the top of the canyon in the usual manner, but Wolf, who customarily leads us into Joonas Halls, is seen crossing the portal marker without leaving the realm. We all try, but to no avail. Wolf suggests that we use the tunnel instead. I have never taken the stone way before, though I am aware it leads to one of the balconies of the Great Hall of the New Guild Center, and that from there we can access Ma-l's realm in many ways. We are about at half the distance when we come across two Angels who quickly vanish through the stone. Wolf claims one of the two is the same that trespassed a week prior. I ask him if he's sure.

"Energy-wise yes," he says. "Look-wise, it moved too fast for me to tell, but I'm pretty sure."

We finally make it to the Center, where we catch a temporary portal to the gathering grounds. Wolf returns to his post at the top of the canyon.

As soon as I get to the kitchen, I tell Angel Liv about the portal incident. She assures me it's just a glitch in the system – other throughways are also acting erratically. Angel Lillian joins in – she heard what I told Liv.

"I am calling Portals to get it fixed, it's been too frequent. At least we have the tunnels as backup," she says.

Angel Khaldun overhears as well.

"Yes, but the tunnel to this realm is closed. If the portals to Joonas Halls fail, we're stuck!" he exclaim.

I refrain from mentioning the little-used corridor to Snake's volcano. At any rate, I let the techs take care of it. My friends and I want to enjoy some of the performances – especially the singers from Xarn's villages.

But then I remember about the two Angels in the tunnel. Before I have a chance to inform Liv, Great One Amaterasu stealthily takes me to the side.

"How is it working with Warrior Xarn?" she asks.

I tell her how much I love his place, and what a joy it is to report from it.

"I was hoping for more of his presence at the gathering – is there anything that I should know about?" she further enquires

"He's not antisocial but he enjoys his privacy. I also believe that he doesn't like leaving the realm unprotected – the Angel intrusion has left him suspicious of the integrity of some of them. As a matter of fact, two passed us on the way here and vanished through what appeared to have been private portals," I answer.

"Thank you, Monique – I shall take care of it. In the meantime you and the villagers enjoy the performances – it's not too late to catch up on some exceptional shows."

She smiles, wishing for us to connect again some time soon.

I sense she wants me to keep the incidence of the tunnel to myself – *ça me satisfait.*

137

35 – REVOLVING DOORS

Place of action: the Great Hall
Date: year 1 of the Realms, G-day 5
Chronicler: Angel Grisha
Department of Warrior and Realm History

———————

Agent Vera's instructions to step back leave no doubts as to what is happening. In the field, it commonly goes by the oxymoron "offensive retreat." The four elders who – as it turns out – work in pairs, have been playing musical chairs. When Vera called, I was just about to follow two of them into the tunnels. I believe they have portals positioned in countless places to help them make the leap from the Center's floor to deep inside the corridors, allowing them to bypass the entryways – when the guards spot them, it's always too late. When within the Great Hall, they can maneuver swiftly from space to space to lose their followers. Because of the vantage afforded by the logistical position of my personal portals, I have been able to partially catch up with their movements. They act fast, so it's difficult to predict where they will come out – but one thing is certain – whatever they're doing is repetitive and rhythmic. It's easy to conclude that they are enacting the same pattern with each passage, albeit in endless permutations – though I am unsure of the purpose behind it, since besides hopping tunnels or hiding in Ma-l's realm, they have nowhere to go but return to the Great Hall.

To the best of my ability, I keep Le Lien informed of their in and outs – again we are dealing with two pairs operating on variations of reduced predictability.

I don't know if others have noticed, but I am under the impression there is a loss of focus to the reality of the Center – it's imperceptible – more like a feeling than a visual observation. I wish Khaldun was on the team to second me on the nuance. At any rate, I share my suspicion with Vera, who is still in the maze. She responds by saying it's why we have to back off – for some reason, the more energy is spent on the search, the more it aggravates the situation. We are now limited to standing still, while the four roam the tunnels like banshees. I don't know how the Moscow reference applies, aside from the waiting game – at least we knew what we were waiting for.

The waiting comes to an abrupt halt when Master Rashnu materializes by my side.

"I see Grisha is kept busy monitoring traffic to and from the gathering," he remarks, as if amused.

"What a coincidence, Angel Rashnu," I say, "I was just thinking about you – you've been hard to reach. I've been looking for you at the cafeteria in hopes of joining your regular morning meetings."

"I'm sorry you've missed on the best part of what was being discussed, but what's to come should give you a fairly good idea of what it was," he teases.

"You see, Master Rashnu, I am not without my personal informants, so the nature of your business is no mystery to some of us. Let me just say that you shouldn't simply assume that you've been operating in a vacuum – this place has eyes," I say.

"Therefore, those eyes should be experiencing blurry vision by now. Don't fool yourself into pretending to know something that you cannot comprehend. Your previous assignment may have been one as a spy in Earth's old Soviet Union – mine, as it stands, is a several millennia-long saga of extreme espionage, aided by the kind of technology you couldn't possibly dream of possessing. I hope your little book gets to document the humiliating collapse of your precious realms," he gloats, as he's about to leave.

But he can't – I guess the school of extreme espionage misplaced a course.

Rashnu's personal portal is disabled by Amaterasu before he has a chance to escape. We are immediately transported to a secured section of Le Lien headquarters, where we are joined by Vac and Vera, freshly back from the tunnels. Masters Jaco and Lo-shen also arrive to take charge of the transfer of the high-profile criminal to the main Guild.

"The technology we couldn't possibly dream of owning, Master Rashnu, is in the process of becoming obsolete. That makes your friend Dzalarhons wrong on two counts," Jaco says. "Personally, I would prefer to have you back in there for you to see for yourself, but you owe much explaining to the Guild. On the other hand, it looks like your accomplices will not enjoy the privilege of the relative painlessness of your predicament. When all settles down, all shall return to stone."

36 – UNSETTLING NUANCES

Zone of nuance: Great Goddess Ma-1's domain
Date: year 1 of the Ma-lean calendar, G-day 6
Chronicler: Angel Khaldun
Honorary member, Department of
Warrior and Realm History

Ma-1's kitchen has turned out to be my favorite spot for documenting the gathering. Of course, I have ventured onto the grounds and spoken with many guests who have voiced their deep appreciation for being part of such a pivotal event. Aside from the incident of the two couples of elders whose energies did not suit the general theme – and perhaps of a few more that skimmed along the borders of my field of perception – I have found that all nuances emanating from the flow of visitors, are sympathetic with the larger vibrational gestalt. Now, I should point that by sympathetic I don't strictly mean harmonious – a fitting discordance, like someone dropping a pile of dishes, or a dog barking during a quiet performance, is part of the natural order. Among the array of apposite dissonances, we find the common tensions associated with the stress of responsibility, such as in the case of the workers, or the occasional frayed nerves that arise from various lesser disagreements. It is my job to be assured of a suitable placement for all these elements. There is no room for misguided assumptions in my field – all must belong to its proper category. Of course, there is a paradox involved when the intuitive is to be corralled – but that is why we call it science. Most of the nuances in question are the byproduct of the interaction of individuals with each other, but the qualitative effect of the relationship between these individuals and their environment also forms an important group – and that is the point I am getting to.

For the last four to five days, I have observed a peculiar shift in the physical makeup that shows minute shearing stress from its spiritual counterpart. As it stands right now, it is about to slip from the definition of nuance to something more obvious. It would be far-fetched to assume it is something more than just one of the growing pains of the realms, but a conspiratorial mind may see otherwise. As an example, some of my colleagues would call it "the overshadowing of a reality by an unforeseen and ominous presence" – in other words, something unpleasant in the making. Perhaps the intermittent malfunctions of the portals foretoken what is to come – but that would be serving intrigue over science.

With that in mind, my job is to find the appropriate box for the energy shift I am presently observing. Some readers may wonder why I do not contact Qwave to investigate – let me just say that Qwave comes to our department when they need to understand something beyond the scope of their instruments. Actually, much of their software is designed by our team – one such program allowed Olaf Swyndle to detect portals in his world. If I were to connect with anyone, it would be Le Lien, but I trust they are already on it – surveillance has a nose for nuances of a certain level of dark intensity.

There are a number of layers of categorization – most notably, cause and purpose. I concern myself with the root of effect, not ideology. Upon closer look, the shift that is distorting the communication between the physical and the spiritual is generated by a combination of inside and outside sources in a symbiotic contract. I now doubt that it is integral to the rapid evolution of the realms – to the contrary – it strongly points in the direction of a systematic undermining of their collective integrity. The overview of the last few days makes it clear that the two couple's odd energy has something to do with it.

I am about to share my findings with Angel Bluefeather when Great One Amaterasu makes eye contact from a distance, indicating she seeks my attention. We meet midway.

"I couldn't help notice you just observed what I have been monitoring for the last few days. As you know, I taught the first class in nuance," she says.

"And I owe my job to you," I reply with pointed gratitude. "Is there anything I should concern myself with?"

"Nothing beyond the boundaries of your field, Angel Khaldun – I recommend that you keep on with the chronicling. I also advise that you use sound judgment before you share your observations with those inclined to – let's say – misinterpret scientific evidence," she returns with a conspiratorial smile.

Point well taken – I almost broke one of the cardinal rules of my department. I guess the role of reporter has me out of my element. I thank the honorable One.

"Nothing to it," she says. "As to the shift, I can affirm your categorization is accurate – but rest assured it is being dealt with in an efficient manner."

She thanks me for my discretion then walks back the way she came. She is gone in the blink of an eye.

37 – A WARRIOR'S PERSPECTIVE

Environment: Warrior Enola's domain
Date: year 1 of the Enolaean calendar, G-day 5
Chronicler: Warrior Enola, Great Goddess

As the one Warrior out of the three fully aware of the act of sabotage affecting the tunnels, Great One Amaterasu and Angel Vac asked me to add a few words to the reports covering Ma-l's celebration. I told them it was Angel Gretchen's job to chronicle from my world's perspective; and that since she had witnessed the intruders' arrest and subjected herself to Le Lien protocol, she was fully capable of representing me and free to wander beyond the artistic side of my creations.

Well, Angel Gretchen as it turns out, is not into what she calls "negative vibes," so I accepted on the one condition that my report be published no matter what, and in its naked entirety.

I was beyond myself when Dzalarhons and Caax trespassed. I took it as an affront to my person and those I had entrusted with the role of guarding my city – namely the villagers from Xarn's realm. When agent Vera and I found the seed programs embedded in the walls of the old tunnel linking my world to the Great Hall, I was once again ready for battle. In spite of my creator status, something awakened the Warrior whose soul became trapped in the stone long ago. I wished those Angels dead – not simply erased from the face of existence – but brought to ruin with my bare hands, until nothing of them was left but a conscious loop of their demise to be replayed for eternity. It took massive control on my part to not unleash those repressed passions, so I apologize to Vera for my bad mood during our search. At least, her presence allowed me to ground instead of throwing my rage at the entire Guild and shutting my doors to the hubs. It is now my understanding that a criminal element by the name of XVII is behind this grave violation inflicted on the collective of the realms and the city of Angels. So, in a way, volunteering for the report is indicative that I am partially over it – but...

Of those who claim they understand what we, Warriors, went through, few have a grip on fully comprehending the nature of psychological desolation. We were buried alive with the ravages of our upbringings, notwithstanding the traumas and humiliations of the lost battles, with no exit for them. The worlds we ended up creating are the results of the torturously long evolution of our dreams into coherent pictures, slowly mated to purposes that rose from so deep, that it felt like with each upward thrust, these fragile images tumbled back into the depths. My city and its surroundings are the products of pain – the colors and the vitality of my vision, the counterpoints to the agony and despair that I thought would never leave me. So when one dares desecrate my work with the blindness of arrogance, it is not just anger that I feel, but the cumulative forces of millennia of imposed paralysis, ready to come free with unrestrained fury.

I am thankfully changed and strengthened by my experience, but the healing is still happening, while moments of fragility are also painfully common – especially when assuming the physical form.

146

This isn't an ultimatum, but the Angel body should make sure it has all of its unwanted characters out of realm reality, before it can pretend to be of help. I was at first honored and rejoiced by the visits, by all the attention that went into my creations; but I am no longer sure I want my world to be perceived as the subject of entertainment for students and Masters on an art kick, or worse: seen as exotic, because it is borne of the alienation I just spoke of.

It would pain me to lose Angel Lev, but the final cost is not always worth the gratification of the moment. I have existed alone for too long, to not have learned to live comfortably with myself. I can do it all as I always have. If I were to close my doors, only the briefest of memory would be left of this moment, a flash of no consequence in the context of infinity and limitless potential. In other words, beyond this very present, Angels and guests from other dimensions of reality, mean absolutely nothing to me. I am my own Oneness in all of its multiplexing expressions – outside realities that seek to infringe on my sacred space, do not merit the courtesy of a memory. I want Dzalarhons and Caax, and all the other dislocated puppets knee-jerking their existences away under the fallacies of ideologies that deny life's greater wisdoms and stifle evolution, to know that. Fanaticism has sent humanity reeling against the grain of common sense for much too long – it saddens me that the same insanities should be present among Angels. My world is the antithesis of all the joys that have been destroyed at the hand of human madness – if my creation must be erased, it will be under my rule.

I seek no apology from any authority. Some of the elders have proven to be despicable characters, while the young roam wide-eyed on the high of one day serving the unknown of uncharted planes of reality. The party may be going on in Ma-l's realm, but in mine, I am left with picking up the pieces – from this point on, visits from the Center are on strict invitational basis.

Of course, this is only relevant if what is happening inside the tunnels can get fixed before it is too late. As the Great Goddess of my realm, I see two opposite developing scenarios – one is, if the guidance of an unlikely hero does not reach its goal of awakening the forces necessary to stop the countdown, the realms will forever be shut from each other and the collective known as the new Oneness will be destroyed, taking with it the old and new system of tunnels, Angel City, the New Guild Center, Joonas Halls, and sadly, Saka and Amaterasu's stones.

So this is my recommendation: if we survive this, the Angels must know that their place here is to learn, and for the Warriors to do the teaching.

It must be time for me to end my tirade, because Angel Gretchen informs me that Great One Amaterasu is seeking to meet with me. I may send a Master away, but never a One.

We spend nearly an hour of my realm's time to go over what has happened. It's now certain the damage in the tunnels is being addressed by no other than Joonas. I feel renewed hopes in my relationship with the Center and my collaboration with Lev. How quickly things turn around – including my own emotional upheavals! What I have written is to remain, even if my mind is in another place after this meeting. As I meant to say when I started – naked words from a naked soul.

38 – AN UNFORTUNATE ERROR OF JUDGMENT

Place of activity: The New Guild Center
Date: year 1 of the Realms, G-day 5
Chronicler: Senior Master Qo'ai-Marael,
Honorary member Department of
Warrior and Realm History

The events of the last few days have been particularly tolling on my person – I shall explain: Masters Jaco and Lo-shen have been kind enough to look the other way, while I should have been the subject of an investigation for my part in pushing for the last group of elders to qualify for admission to the Assembly, and eventually the realms. I have always known about XVII, because I was offered to join when Dzalarhons left the original team at the time of the consolidation of the families into the Guild. We used to be extremely close; we attended the first meeting together. Sadly, the numeric of their name reflects my presence then, and has remained an indelible mark on my conscience ever since. Even though I never technically joined, I always felt somewhat affiliated with the group, to the point of concealing vital information about their actions. Regrettably, some of it pertained to what is now developing in the realms; hence, I can no longer hide behind the mask of deceit. To a vast extent, I am responsible for the madness that is being played out in

150

the tunnels – in that regard, I may never forgive myself. Had I handed what I knew then to *Third Eye*, and later, Le Lien, none of this would be happening, and those fighting to save the realms would instead be enjoying their rightful place at the gathering. I also was aware of the work of Angels Jen and Lawrence – I could have tipped Portals about their deeds, but I kept silent to protect my shame. When Master Lo-shen asked me to spy on Jaco, I sensed it was a trap. Had I known he wasn't part of XVII, I might have answered differently. I never was an active member though, which partially explains why I was left alone during the sweep and the deportation of the suspects that ensued from the emergency meeting. Perhaps my turn is still yet to come.

It is clear I was used by XVII. The group exploited my weakness, one of love for Dzalarhons. She and I were once partners – it happened not long after she left the first team, and while my heart was still sore from a painful breakup with my longtime work partner, whose name I am not at liberty to divulge. Among humans, we would have been a lesbian couple. We grew apart because of our philosophical differences, but my love for her never waned. I now finally realize that Dzalarhons avenged herself for the severance, by taking advantage of my deep-rooted guilt for having instigated it. The whole thing is a Greek tragedy that could have been easily avoided if my head had been properly screwed on my shoulders.

When Dzalarhons begged of me to fit XVII into the last batch of Angels to volunteer for the realms, I couldn't say no, even in the light of the monumental implications of that choice. I am fully complicit of the act of treason that has been committed; thus, I must come face to face with my own conscience for the final judgment.

I saw Dzalarhons one last time as she was being hauled away. Our eyes crossed. I swear I saw twisted glee in that look of hers – a victorious and vindictive final arrow sent straight through my heart. It said it all with irrevocable precision – the entire course of events from our breakup onwards, pivoted on my inherent weakness of character.

I ask for forgiveness from the reader, should he or she be made aware of the insincerities of my previous reports. I ask for forgiveness from the Guild and the Great God and Goddesses of the realms, for jeopardizing their chances to exist in harmony. I hope from the depths of my heart, that Amaterasu can weather the winds of my betrayal. To all – I am sorry, Q-M

39 – CRITICAL POINT

Place of action: the Great Hall
Date: year 1 of the Realms, G-day 6
Chronicler: Angel Grisha
Department of Warrior and Realm History

Rashnu's arrest is testament to the eight XVII operatives' drive to act as if they had nothing to lose. Their plan was reckless, bordering on suicidal. They didn't try to hide – to the contrary – they provoked. I ask myself, "what did they have to gain from the sabotage of the realms?" but I cannot find an answer beyond madness gone madder from feeding at the trough of fanaticism. It had to come from way back, when the Guild was just a concept – but what in the realms threatened Dzalarhons and the other sixteen original members, to the point that they wished for their demise? I can only come to the one conclusion that – unlike what I first thought – it was personal reasons rather than ideology that drove those passions. I don't believe it's a stretch to assume Dzalarhons' antagonism is aimed at Great One Amaterasu – she's the one who has all to lose from the collapse of the realms and the end of the power of the stones. As members of the original team, I wonder if the two Angels weren't competing for the attention of the Oneness – or rather – if Dzalarhons wasn't envious of Amaterasu's relationship with *it*. After all, the rise of the realms as an autonomous and complementary reality, was the pivotal element to that closeness. It's also rumored the stones were a gift of the One – it's all tied in.

I realize I am caught in my own thinking process, when Master Qo'ai-Marael joins me by the entrance to Snake's world, located on the floor below the Great Hall. The events of the last few days have left visible marks on the Angel's aura – I don't believe she is doing well.

"Hello, Grisha, still mixing work with pleasure?" she mildly humors.

"You have cracked the mystery of my person, Master, but I trust you are not here to talk about me," I say.

"Indeed – I seek a favor. If I were to walk right in there," (she points to the tunnel,) "could I have your word that you will not report the act to Le Lien – at least not until the end of the day?"

"Why should I? I am only keeping an eye on the movements of the last three remaining elders, who are still believed to be opening links and placing seeds in the maze. I may chronicle your moves for the history department, but I have no valid reason to report you to Le Lien so far, unless you convince me otherwise." I tell her.

"Thank you, Grisha."

Those are her last words before she enters the tunnel. Surprisingly, no guard is present.

I soon forget about the incident, because something is happening with the light and the sharpness around me. I decide to visit with Spencer who's at Le Lien on the level below.

Lillian lets me in. There is a meeting going on with Liv, Vac, Vera, Spencer, Ilia, Axel, Jaco, Lo-shen, Enola, Amaterasu, as well as two Qwave techs. I don't have to tell the reader something of importance is unfolding. The team updates me on Joonas. I am also told we are steadily losing the realms, as the first perceptible signs have been felt in various parts of the Center. The system of common portals used to connect with Joonas Halls and the domains of the Warriors, is also starting to fail. It is estimated that by tomorrow, the seeds will have merged into a single controlling force that will reactivate the old tunnels and shut everything else, resulting in the entombment of the New Guild Center with everyone in it.

Was it Vera who asked me to act as if I still were on my last assignment on Earth? "Pretend you're back in Moscow," I believe she had said. Well, this is more like acting in a Hollywood spy movie, with its sets of caves and tunnels, while villains are on the loose... – no such thing while interminably waiting on the Red Square under freezing November rains. Our situation here is countdown-critical. It's like choosing which wire to cut to disable a bomb – in an instant it could all be gone.

"So, what has Joonas to lose if he fails?" I ask.

Vac answers.

"Technically, Joonas has all to gain. Putting our trust in him may appear to be pure folly, but that's the nature of the paradox. The elements must play at their own level. There is little doubt Amaterasu could stop it all, but Dzalarhons knew that she wouldn't – it's in the hands of different players. So far, no stone has been left unturned – so we wait for the last minute heroes to act their parts. It's not that Joonas is not to be trusted as much as it is whether he can do the job by himself or not. There may be one actor we are overlooking."

That's when I remember what Qo'ai-Marael asked of me – to not inform Le Lien of her presence in the tunnels. She entered the new system anyway, but can she possibly have knowledge of the links between old and new? I'm an Angel of my word – I will only let the team know at the end of the day.

40 – CROSSED FINGERS

Place of action: the New Guild Center
Date: year 1 of the realms, G-day 6
Chronicler: Angel Vera, team Le Lien,
Guild archivist

I'm not going to pretend it's not nerve-racking to find yourself at the epicenter of the imminent collapse of the realms. Sure, the Warriors will carry on in their individual domains, disconnected from each other for who knows how long – but without the lane of the stones, we, Angels, are in dire straits. It's complicated because even without potential for growth, whatever exists of the new Oneness is still a separate gestalt from the original One. It means we're stuck in the Hall for eternity! Our physical bodies will – like all things mortal – be reclaimed by time. But our ghosts will dwell these spaces like souls with no other place to go – not your top-drawer forecast.

When Vac says it's now time for the last minute heroes to act their parts, I'm under the impression he knows more than the rest of us – save for Amaterasu. Who could the other players be, besides Joonas's useless gang of drunks against three frantic Angels downloading self-cloning seeds at every turn of the maze? Right now, based on the dimming lights – the ubiquitous glows we all have come to accept as the Center's gauge for vitality – complete with erratic portals et al – it doesn't appear Joonas has much of a grip on the situation. Grisha's question is potent – yes, what does he have to lose? Vac puts a lot of trust into the Hektor founder, as if his past was of no consequence. We all are aware of the importance of opposite forces within the emergence of all events, but how does one know where the tipping point is when dealing with linear reality? Of course, we all also understand that probabilities offer a variety of outcomes dependent on how the present plays out, but the realms don't talk much in that department. Vac assures us that no stone has been left unturned. I assume he's correct, because we did all we could – including backing off from doing anything at all. Talk about a loaded paradox!

Tomorrow is the last day of the gathering – perhaps we can all go out with a bang. In honor of Ma-l and Xarn, we had planned – actually it was Bluefeather's idea – a clothing-optional finale, including dancing around bonfires; a Midsummer festival – realm-style.

I know it hasn't been discussed, but I'm sure some have thought about it: what stops us, Angels, from splitting the assembly into three groups and moving into the realms before all goes to hell? Problem is, Enola is the only Warrior with the lowdown. Since we're all still in the room, I ask her.

"Well, you don't have much of a choice," she replies. "I'm not exactly enthusiastic about it, but I can't let you rot in your cave."

That was tactful.

"As far as Ma-l's concerned, most of the Angels will already be in her realm when the tunnels and the portals shut down. She will be stuck with you, and you can explain then – she may get over it with time," she adds.

"How do you reconcile the fact you and Xarn might also be locked in her world?" I ask.

"Just aspects of our greater consciousnesses. Remember, we never leave our realms – we are the realms," she says firmly.

"What will happen of Xarn and Saka?" I ask Vac.

"Saka is now a Goddess; she'll figure it out," he answers.

"Are you implying that somehow the Warriors will find a way to connect?" I pry.

"The old lanes will be alive even if controlled by an entity that doesn't wish for them to be connected – if that's indeed what the plan is. Potential for connection will always be there – it's an integral and inseparable law of the collective embedded in each of the realms. Simply said – the whole cannot exist without its parts and vice versa."

"So eventually, we could all return to old Angel City?" I probe.

"In time's terms, it could mean in an eternity – but yes, XVII's deeds will be reclaimed by evolution," he says.

"So we have nothing to worry about," I chance.

"Technically not, but there is an unsolvable item with this one course, in that our humans guests cannot remain in Ma-l's reality – all their foreseeable developments exist outside the realms. That's why there has to be another actor involved," he adds.

That's when Grisha comes forward with the news. He explains he had to wait to honor his promise but that it is now time for him to speak. We hear about Master Qo'ai-Marael's entrance into Snake's tunnel. I figure there is no point to it, but then Lo-shen comes forward and clarifies on the Master's position with XVII and her tragic affair with Dzalarhons. She was meant to eventually be apprehended and returned to the Guild for evaluation, but *Third Eye* wanted to give her room to manœuvre, just in case she would come face to face with the paradigm she had created for herself. As it turns out, it was one of Vac's many suggestions as a consultant to Le Lien – both Jaco and Lo-shen agreed to wait.

My head spins – I'm still in Earth mode from the case back in Humboldt. I've got to get back to Ma-l's kitchen and get stoned with Saka. I'm much better at field work than sitting around, waiting while rationalizing about the reasons why we're not doing anything.

That's when the lights brighten and everything comes back into focus.

"Our last hero has spoken; George's ghost image is no more," Amaterasu says. "We can all return to whatever we were doing before this all came down. Enjoy the celebration, you deserve it," she adds, before she leaves with Vac and Sam.

Well, that was a quick turnaround.

I'm off to Ma-l's place to get reunited with my friends in the kitchen. Hopefully Bluefeather and I can spend the night in some nest overlooking the valley.

My return doesn't get unnoticed – the host greets me like an old friend she hasn't seen in a long time.

"Are things alright?" Ma-l asks as if she always knew.

"I wasn't so certain until a moment ago, but I can assure you they couldn't be any better," I return, donning the classic smile of one who gets to the limelight after having narrowly averted disaster.

41 – THE FINAL DAY

Place of activity: Great Goddess Ma-l's domain
Date: year 1 of the Ma-lean calendar, G-day 7
Chronicler: Angel Bluefeather
Department of Warrior and Realm History

It's nice to see everyone present. The last week has been more like a revolving door between Joonas Halls and Ma-l's grounds. There is a distinctly easy flow this morning, as if the elements had just awakened with renewed hopes – I sense love is in the air. My suggestion to go all bare has yielded minimal interest, but the day is still young. Me, I walk my talk. Vera will join in later – she's up in our private hideaway enjoying a break from the action. Lillian and Geir have already assumed their posts in the kitchen, while Pau and Marshall are in the garden picking beans. Xarn is making a rare appearance, meeting with Saka who seems to be absorbed in deep meditation out on the grass.

Angels Niamh and Tealsky have not been seen since my brief interaction with them on day two – but neither have I noticed the presence of many of the loveless elders from the last arrival. Angel Emile, on the other hand, has been kind enough to entertain us with many stories from some of his most extreme assignments. One thing I can attest to is that whoever hangs out in the kitchen, knows a thing or two about heart connections. It doesn't matter what species you belong to, or what level of evolution you stand at – if you seek the warmth of stove tops and brick ovens, your heart and soul are drawn to love and the comfort of others. The kitchen is where laughter and unbridled pleasures reign unchallenged – it is the place for Geir and Lillian, Khaldun, Emile, Vera, and I. For the romantics, it will be the gardens or the swimming holes of the creek – a different kind of emotional charge. But one doesn't exclude the other – different times, different moods – it's all about healthy connections.

I am witnessing an influx of villagers from Xarn's realm. I am told some of them came from as far as the sea at the mouth of the great river that runs along the bottom of the God's home canyon. I am mesmerized by both their uniqueness and the boundless love that emanates from their beings – a deep, virgin self-love that touches everyone around them. I expected to see so many more of them earlier, but I sense they weren't ready – or that something prevented them from crossing over. Interestingly enough, their presence is inversely proportional to the absence of elders – I wonder if there's a connection. I guess it's another question for my good friend Khaldun who just happens to be nearby.

"Yes, there is one, Bluefeather," he says. "Their diametrically opposite energies simply cannot co-exist. I have no idea where those elders went, but I hope they never return – there was an aura of apocalyptic foreboding about them."

"Yes, someone was joking about a Hektor convention a few days ago," I humor.

"For a second, I admit I had my doubts, but it appears it's now water over the dam. I'm off for a swim in the creek – feel like joining?" Khaldun offers,

I politely decline. I am waiting for Vera – today my heart is in realm mode, if you get the drift.

I observe Great One Amaterasu and Master Vac walking toward Enola and Lev who are attending to one of the stages. I wonder if anyone will ever know of the Great One and the Angel's status as a couple. Of course Vac is assuming the dog guise, so the idea of a sexual relationship between them forms an odd concept – but Vac has not always been a dog. I remember him in one of his many human shapes – but then again, none of us are human to start with. We all know there's deep-rooted spiritual connection between them – a bond so strong that it's difficult to imagine their energies separate from each other. It has been speculated that they are the original primary elements – the male and female, the plus and minus inherent to all of existence, physical and not – the first gestalts of consciousness free to explore away from the Oneness. From my perspective, it amounts to a lot of love!

Here comes Vera in all of her naked glory. I notice many a garb has fallen all around since my last mention – we're on a good start!

Today, all the chroniclers are to gather to collaborate on an end piece for the reports. Actually, I will suggest that we first enjoy the celebration as a team, and then work on the conclusion in a couple of days – I don't think the department will object. Beautiful Angels Monique and Gretchen are finally seen together on the grounds, after having been mostly attached to Enola and Xarn's realms.

"Bonjour mes demoiselles," I venture.

"Tag!" Gretchen counters.

I take it that French charm amid pastoral settings isn't going to get me anywhere. We settle for sitting with the others in the mid-afternoon sun. I hear for the first time that Enola had been invited to write a piece – I was not aware Spencer was partaking either – the more the merrier!

"Circumstance dictates," I hear Vera interject.

It is clear something other than the celebration is being chronicled – but everything in its due time. It is a beautiful day and no cloud bigger than the purple-bottomed puffballs that sparsely dot the sky is allowed.

Vera takes my arm and pulls me in the direction of the creek – the kitchen will wait.

42 – CLOSING REPORT FROM KHALDUN

Zone of nuance: Great Goddess Ma-l's domain
Date: year 1 of the Ma-lean calendar, G-day 7
Chronicler: Angel Khaldun
Honorary member, Department of
Warrior and Realm History

I find the perfect quiet spot by the creek. I need the serene effect of the running water and the play of splashes against the rounded rocks. As the registrar of nuances, I have learned to shield myself from the influence of what one may call "negative energy." It is of course a matter of perspective, as we all know that much is created from the self. Nonetheless, the physical experience, as chosen for the celebration, is prone to emotional fluctuations that can often spike in impromptu fashion. I'm here to ground the superfluous energy that broke through the guards.

It is evident by the clarity of the moment, that the darkness that hovered above the grounds is now gone. The group of elders responsible for it has also left with it. I have no doubt that the sporadic absence of the Le Lien team from the kitchen is tied to it. I have tried to investigate, but I was advised to stay close to my work instead. I am confident all will be brought to the light in due time.

That being said, my field provides room for the deductive process to be used without crossing the line into assumptions. The elders came with an agenda which marred the general tone of the gathering. Their motives were of nefarious nature – I have no doubt about it. I am an expert in defining the various elements that formed into the collective aura of Hektor, and none of what I read in the elders matches any of them. I conclude we are in the presence of a different group with a unique energy signature. The fact that only members of original families of Angels carried that energy, indicates that such an organization is – in time's terms – ancient. Additionally, their intentions – by targeting the realms – bring the formation of the group to the era of, at least, the Great Battles. The glaring fact that all of them worked on distant assignments explains why they remained unnoticed. So why have Masters Jaco, Emile and Lo-shen – who have been seen with the others – not been channels of those ominous winds?

The reader may ask why I bother with details that will eventually be revealed – the answer is simple: it's a test of accuracy. I have a duty towards my field to come up with answers that match facts, based on the deductive process. Short of better words, I'm a passive investigator – meaning, I am not tied to a case – but technically, I am fine- tuning an area that could eventually serve Le Lien. At their raw end, nuances are similar to the stuff of intuition – refined, they are a science. Of course, others, such as Lo-shen, Amaterasu, and Vac are masters in the field – it is how they decide to act or not on issues, how they define what belongs to the primary evolutionary course and what must be triaged in the direction of probable outcomes.

No need to dwell on the tedious details, but the latest nonattendance by Qo'ai-Marael leaves me perplexed. After all, she is the one who authorized the transfer of the last group, and she also was part of the original team with Joonas and Dzalarhons – plus, she was the head historian in the Guild and is now at the helm of the department here. Her energy was never dark though – more like a neutral grey – but it doesn't mean she isn't compromised. I cannot perceive nuances from someone who's not in my field of reception, but I can extrapolate on a previous reading to see how it develops in the context of time already passed. Last I saw her, she was speaking with Bluefeather, before he joined Niamh and Tealsky. There was confusion, which I assigned to an overextended schedule, but there was also the turquoise of hope in her auratic space, almost as if she counted on Bluefeather to fix something broken.

Now let's see how it evolves from there...

Just when Bluefeather leaves with Jaco and Lo-shen, the turquoise of hope is washed away by a wave that leaves only the dull yellow grey of the sand. The light dims, as clouds mask the sun. There are strong whirling winds that push the billowing masses in all directions, before they dissipate as if recalled from the scenery by a reluctant painter. The sun sets a deep orangey-red over the calm sea. Later, as the stars disappear one by one, electric storms rip the skies at unpredictable intervals – she is not in control of her destiny – very unusual for an elder Master of her stature. I don't need to go much further to understand blackmail is involved – the emotional kind. She is being manipulated, and the nuance points straight to Dzalarhons. I read multiple layers simultaneously – the crimson red of envy directed at the highest power catches my attention. There is something very ancient to it – a broken alliance that turns brothers and sisters into mortal enemies. Qo'ai-Marael is shamelessly used by Dzalarhons to get to that power. The realms sit in the middle of the struggle. I believe the historian has the means to stop it all, but the reasons she refrains are masked by a shadow that grows darker with time. The causes do not interest me – I now simply wait for the facts to come into the light.

–Angel Khaldun–

43 – CLOSING REPORT FROM GRETCHEN

Place: Great Goddess Ma-l's domain
Date: year 1 of the Ma-lean calendar, G-day 7
Chronicler: Angel Gretchen
Department of Warrior and Realm History

––––––––––––

My time in GG-Enola's domain has taught me much about the creational elements of art. Our commutes into GG-Ma-l's realm have also highlighted how tied these worlds are to each other and how compatible they are in accepting input from one another. I have taken many notes about my work setting up the stages and maneuvering around the performances, plus many more about the diversity at the base of the energy of the celebration – I gather now is the time to put some order into them.

There is no need to further explore the intense passion behind GG-Enola's work – let it be said that she is as much driven by anger as she is by delight – that is what contributes to the vibrancy in her creations. The pains of repression and injustice don't lie – when expressed innovatively, the joys that ensue are proportional to the authenticity of the output. The Goddess' art is as alive as her constantly-whirling passions – it doesn't take long to figure that out about her.

Until the point of the intrusion into her realm, GG-Enola was über-exited about working with Angel Lev on setting up the décor for the gathering grounds. After it, her involvement became sporadic, as she trusted the young Master with his own skills. Her mind was preoccupied with matters that had cast a shadow over her creative self – she was defensive, protective of her space to the point of shutting her realm to visitors. Her passions were to no longer cater to the dreams and the creative, but rather to survival and the protection of all that was dear to her – she was ready for battle. She had been brought to the point at which the forces of destruction met those of creation. It worried me for the union of the realms. The trespassing carried the intension of disrupting the harmony between us, Angels and Warriors. I saw what Enola did to Caax and Dzalarhons – I don't think they expected it.

I refrained from chronicling for a while – my mind was not into it. My preoccupations went to regrouping the energy that was scattered by the impact of the incident. I am drawn to art as a form of expression which I see – even at its darkest moments – as a positive force. What happened then, was far from constructive – it challenged my comfort zone, which is to surround myself with all I consider beautiful, including the elements of tragedy immortalized through creative release. So I went on to document GG-Enola's city, as well as its bordering desert and semi-desert wilderness, as a means to distance myself from what I sensed was a storm building up in the background of the celebration. I knew too much and I couldn't cope with it. I was briefed by kind souls on remaining silent about what I had witnessed, and it suited where I was at emotionally. When the Goddess asked me if I wanted to extend my report beyond art, meaning sharing my views on the intrusion for the history department, I recoiled to the safety of my original assignment. She resigned herself to be the one to chronicle her thoughts on the subject. For a second, I felt I was going to be asked out of her world – but it was just me being fragile at the time. I may appear cold to the outsider, but it's a cover that I inherited from my last assignment in wartime Nazi Germany as a nurse – I never went through a proper rehabilitation phase when I reentered the Guild; instead, I opted for the realms in hope of finding healing grounds. The apparitions of Masters Dzalarhons and Caax came as a shocking reminder of the darkness that drives certain entities to manipulate through the use of logical fallacies and other calculated means of confusing those they seek to exploit. I promise myself to connect with Angels Shade and Shido who have taken over the reentry program, in conjunction with helping the students that fell to Hektor.

Since then, I have been following Angel Lev around as he catered to the needs of the performers, especially the colorful villagers of G-God Xarn. Some of the students' acts were – should I say – too progressive for my tastes. Post-industrial punk affects me in ways that reconnect me to the traumas of my last work on Earth. On the other hand, the revolving singing of the goodness-bound artists from the villages, brings forth much soothing. Based on the perception it took thousands of Earth's years for music to evolve from octave to dominant harmonies, it is easy to imagine how these singers may be bringing the dissonances of the past into the perfect harmonies of the future. The human mind can only take as much as its evolution dictates – or rather – its willingness to evolve beyond set boundaries. But the subject of humanity is best left to the historians and the geneticists.

In few words, I am entranced by the beauty of these people and I commend G-God Xarn on his sacred abilities

172

to bring forth such humble majesty in its extraordinarily expressed form – I am deeply moved. One may see these villagers as the active equivalents to GG-Enola's passive forms – or perhaps a freed version of her captive art. But my words may be too limiting, for there is much freedom in the Goddess' work.

Overall – and at the exception of the odd energy that hovered on and off above the celebration – the patronage has been first class. Angels, humans, Great Ones, Great Goddesses and Gods, villagers – all existing within the same auspicious environment – represent, as a whole, a painting of rare nuances. I am honored to have been part of those allowed to experience the event from the inside – I will cherish that unique perspective forever.

–Angel Gretchen–

44 – CLOSING REPORT FROM MONIQUE

Location: Great Goddess Ma-l's domain
Date: year 1 of Ma-lean calendar, G-day 7
Chronicler: Angel Monique, genetics
Department of Warrior and Realm History

Skatu, Jessie, Alice, and I are totally enthralled by the shows. The three villagers are particularly awed by some of the Angels' performances. I am not sure to what extent they comprehend the hardcore music played by some of the younger students, but they express their appreciation. They are very receptive to creative output in all of its forms. On the other hand, they are only minimally curious about the darker energies that don't belong to that process. On one of my rare visits with Gretchen, the Angel confessed that she found the villagers incapable of interacting with anything that did not fall within the scope of *collective positivity*. When I asked her to explain, she simply theorized that Xarn's people – and possibly his entire realm – were born of an environment devoid of the extremes of most common dualities – and that she believed the paradox only existed at the observer's end. In other words, what she is trying to say is that Xarn's world knows of no negative as universally observed, and that the God himself shepherds that duality away from his creations. It is an interesting concept that challenges much of what I hold as true, but one that I must validate all the same. Then again, to imply the realms represent a unique environment with nearly incomprehensible laws, would be an understatement. Of course, all of this applies mostly to the physical.

For some reason that was not explained to me, Xarn is now allowing visitors into his domain, while he is also being seen at the gathering. Mind you, it's the last day, though I suspect other factors contribute to his change of stance. I was expecting a lot more interaction between the realms, more portals that would have allowed for a better interchange. I am sorry to have to conclude that the greater reasons for the restrictions were caused by the Angels themselves. It is inadmissible that attempts at trespassing were committed by some of us – how very un-Angel-like. I don't have the details, but who else apart from us could have known how to use the tunnels – certainly not the humans. It goes without saying that Amaterasu and the few Great Ones who briefly attended, are incapable of such an act. I sincerely hope these matters are now resolved.

The status quo has left me unable to gather a greater perspective on the celebration – I was only permitted to travel with the villagers who brought supplies over. I was not granted a portal of my own, but Xarn made it clear I had the choice of staying or leaving – as all know, I would not have wanted it any other way.

The role of a Guild geneticist is not defined by classic laboratory research or even field work per se. I study creational variations based on unique algorithms in line with purpose – or put more simply – I keep an eye on the evolution of species in the physical sphere. The main particularity of Xarn's people, is that they don't exist within the conventional *atmosphere* within which we have been operating for countless millennia. The realms evolve on a reversed creational motif, since the Warriors are human-based and their worlds are, essentially, images of their previous realities, carrying with them the auratic blueprint of their individual experiences. What I observe in the God's realm, is the absence of the ego. The villagers do not operate from the strict focus of a shared consciousness either – they can be both individually and collectively-leaning without blurred lines or conflicts. In other words, Xarn's realm represents the closest I have seen of the marriage of the spiritual and the physical, yet in a form that is unique to this emerging Oneness. Simply stated, the classic villager is a spiritual entity – not in the flesh – but in *its* absolute form, one that is seamlessly connected to its environment. Xarn's people are without a doubt, the centers of their own universes, best defined as emergent, free creators of their own – an observation that parallels the model of the original Earth settlers, when the spiritual first assumed the flesh in dizzying variations. But based on my studies and the characteristics of their genetic makeup, the villagers are immune to the "necessary flaws" that defined the Warriors' native reality.

To summarize my work here, I conclude that the realms – as seen from Xarn's domain – represent a unique take on the physical theme, one that bypasses a number of phases of Earth's evolution. Angel Gretchen believes that the *in-body* expression of the worlds of the Warriors, is pure creational art for love's sake.

Quel bonheur !

–Angel Monique–

45 – CLOSING REPORT FROM GRISHA

Place of action: Great Goddess Ma-l's domain
Date: year 1 of the Ma-lean calendar, G-day 7
Chronicler: Angel Grisha
Department of Warrior and Realm History

I never thought I would get a taste of old-school spying while reporting on the celebration, but here we are. I joined the new history department as the result of my wish to settle in a quiet environment after my last mission. I am not immune to trauma – the old USSR was a challenge of unforeseen magnitude, for I am still bearing the weight of it. Actually, from where I stand, I see a number of Angels who have opted for the realms as a means to walk away from the traps of their dominant qualifications. To be a Master of service is a lot like acting in films – one gets locked in a characterial formula. I guess old habits are not easy to shake off.

It is my understanding that we, chroniclers, are meant to cover the gathering from as many angles as possible. My role in the Great Hall is essentially to monitor traffic and document its fluctuations. It is also to record the effects of this symbolic moment on the workings of the New Guild Center; how the heightened energy, the intoxicating emanation of joy play at the larger level.

Though I attest to a general sense of excitement around the event, I was drawn early to the darker influence of the XVII group, and sidetracked from my original task. I have no doubt the final draft of this series of reports will be quite different from its intended purpose. The realms offer a reduced aperture in assessing foreseeable futures, so it's somewhat refreshing to operate from the standpoint of not knowing the variables. In Earth's terms, Dzalarhons and her cohort came from left field. While the nefariousness of their intentions is bound to add spice to the very root history of this emergence, XVII's timing could not have been more inappropriate – yet, there is an absolute to it that makes me wonder to what extent it acts a contributing role to the emancipation process. It's a question for Great One Amaterasu to answer.

I am about to join the grand gathering, where all chroniclers are meeting to go over their notes – except for Qo'ai-Marael of course, who's now finding her peace in the darkness of the old lanes. She did what she had to do – her name remains unmarred.

I am left with the discomforting realization that the presence of Angels in the realms has done absolutely nothing to secure their safety – to the contrary, we have contributed to much disruption since Olaf and Vac first walked into Ma-l's domain. Yet, it is an irrevocable fact that without the work of Masters, these realms would not exist at all. The original One was borne of a dilemma – nothing much different about this emergence, I guess. But then again, I am looking at it from the standpoint of my experience, one much tainted by subjective evaluation.

In conclusion, I ask for the New Guild to take a step back and have a good look at where it stands. The Hall is meant to accommodate its presence outside the gates of the realms, but nowhere does it stipulate that such a presence should ever be necessary inside them – that is for the

Warriors to decide. For the record, we are merely envoys from Guild Headquarters, attached to a new world that might or not need our engineering skills to solidify and maintain the links between its many facets. From where I stand, it doesn't look like the three Warriors are requiring much beyond some occasional company. Olaf is now Ma-l's partner – his Angel status means little. Vac is also attached to the Goddess' realm – but the relationship, again, has little contractual value. As to Lev and Great Goddess Enola, it once more looks like a match of the heart. I believe it's going to be a long time before Angels find themselves in a place where they will be able to act beyond their status as guests. In the meantime, there is much we can learn from the Warriors and their creations – the closer we get to comprehend the realms, the lesser the risk of committing the kinds of mistakes that saw the rise of Hektor and XVII. It is also my humble opinion that the Guild – as a whole – has to take an honest look at itself and contemplate the likelihood of other fissures within its makeup. While the separation was clear with Hektor, the festering of Dzalarhons' group in the background of day to day operation, is a reminder that things are not always as they appear. I concern myself with traffic between the two Onenesses; hence, I beg for this assembly to screen its members for truth and commitment. In my capacity as a fresh Le Lien recruit, I am forever keeping an eye on the portals in and out of this Hall – consider it my pledge of allegiance to the realms.

–Angel Grisha–

46 – CLOSING REPORT FROM SPENCER

Area of activity: Great Goddess Ma-l's domain
Date: year 1 of the Ma-lean calendar, G-day 7
Chronicler: Angel Spencer, team Le Lien

―――――――――

I'll be brief. I wasn't one of the original chroniclers, but the last string of developments has put me in the necessary position to forward transparency in regard to Le Lien's process – Amaterasu greatly approved of the decision. The report of the celebration, as it was presented to me, is technically a commemorative piece of realm emergence. The history department, with Qo'ai-Marael at its helm, deemed it appropriate to immortalize the event in a published work that could reach and entertain the most sentient of species out in the original Oneness, as well as serve as a personal reminder to the realm Angels, of what it was to be there. Again, all of this will appear in the context of time for the reader of the physical sphere.

The infiltration of XVII is a vital lesson for those of us who considered vigilance unnecessary in the New Guild Center, on the view that Angels are without reproach. I would prefer it that way, but most of us here at Le Lien, have had to deal with Hektor's wrongdoings for the last couple of millennia. We have often been accused by extreme thinkers, of fermenting the cases assigned to the team. Frankly, I find it in poor taste to be shown such disloyalty in the face of our dedication to firmness through gentleness. Take Lillian, Vera, and Liv – there are no souls more peaceful than theirs. The fact is that as far as the Guild is concerned, goodness of intent will always come with a shadow side – not necessarily from the same being – but certainly from within the context of its greater environment. We don't profess negativity – we deal with it neutrally by realigning it with its positive counterpart. No force is ever used. As far as the rogue Angels are concerned, when faced with the inevitability of their arrests, their own energy – as it bounced off the greater forces that stood before them – created the shackles that bound them. It was possibly somewhat different with Enola, but her actions were in line with the laws of her realm – let's call it a final lesson for Dzalarhons and Caax, who had the impunity to put the Goddess below them.

On some level, I don't understand why Jaco and Lo-shen didn't contact Le Lien to warn us of XVII's intentions earlier. But I am assured that full disclosure will be made available. I don't doubt that from *Third Eye*'s standpoint, scenarios were limited.

I am above all delighted that the gathering followed its planned course, uninterrupted by what went on in the tunnels. Many of us at Le Lien – and just to name a few – Liv, Vera, Lillian, Stefan, and The Triad have seen the realms' array of possible outcomes, as limited as they might be, flash before our eyes as we worked ahead of Joonas's every moves back on Earth, along Marshall and Geir's timeline. One may say that we, Angels, deities, and humans collectively defeated the shadow side of the Hektor founder and saved the realms. Most precisely, we all stuck together along the course of the best probable scenario. I am particularly grateful for the opportunity to have seen the gates of relation open between groups of various levels of evolution, in the form of a great leap in inter-connective consciousness. To be able to say in the same breath that Marshall, Geir, Ma-l, Olaf, and Amaterasu are my friends, is testament to how much was accomplished in so little time. Needless to say that without all the parts – as infinitesimal as they may be – none of this would have happened. It all hinged on everyone pulling their weight on cue in the absence of a script – bravo!

As to the members of XVII, Vac has informed me that there is talk of them being moved to the realms of Hektor. Dahbar is welcoming all Guild "defects" to his extremely remote fiefdom – to what purpose, I cannot tell – but Tömör is already there and on his way to rehabilitation. I wish them all the best with their new world – I am certain though that they will not enjoy the opportunity to rise against Hektor. Some lessons do indeed come with just the right pinch of irony.

–Angel Spencer–

47 – CLOSING REPORT FROM VERA

Place of action: Great Goddess Ma-l's domain
Date: year 1 of the Ma-lean calendar, G-day 7
Chronicler: Angel Vera, team Le Lien,
Guild archivist

Here we have it – all of us, minus Qo'ai-Marael, finally gathered under one roof. Tons of action here! From the look of it, the attendance is at its apex – we have reached full capacity. Ma-l is radiant – she pulled it off.

Yes, a great weight has lifted – the realms are now truly free to explore their unique potential.

There is much writing on the wall for the New Guild, but the underlying argument – in spite of the general enthusiasm – is to be patient and give the Warriors plenty of elbow room. We're here to learn – period.

This is no business – we're a big family, so we need to act like one. I am fairly certain some of our volunteers will have to face the prospect of returning to their respective places in the main Guild – the realms are for those whose hearts have now melded with the everyday life of the New Center. Until recently, I wasn't so sure where I belonged, but the latest events have sealed it for me. As long as there will be a bridge between the two Onenesses, the potential for disruption will always exist. Le Lien needs to build a stronghold in the Hall to protect the worlds of the Warriors from outside influences. There has been talk of leaving this new universe alone and closing the Center, but Amaterasu is quick to point that Angels are integral to the reality of the realms. All I know is that we can't bring old habits to the table – it's time to learn new tricks. Of course, much is still to come. Each domain is likely to come with its own field of unknowns – and there's a whole hundred and twenty-nine of them left. In the end, there's no doubt we'll come out of it much changed.

I don't know if this was shared in other reports, but just in case it wasn't, let me try to explain: the realms are at a far more linear stage than the Oneness whence we came. Because of it, and in conjunction with their relative newness, we cannot operate backwards from the standpoint of future probable events and observe their individual courses. This unique world is pure, open potential with no defined trajectory. It's not like it doesn't have a future – it's more like it hasn't made up its mind about what it wants for one – primarily because it depends on the unopened realms to map the paths of probabilities from the perspective of the whole. Instead of foreseeable alternatives, we have what can be best described as "educated speculation" – and we know how "reliable" that is... I am not saying that within each realm, there are no probable outcomes – there's no doubt in my mind their creators aren't bound to time, and that they're aware of the many possibilities before them. All I mean to say is that from the place of Angels, we deal with an enigma. Before the realms came untethered, we could to some extent, read into various scenarios – but within them we're essentially blind.

OK, I think I've said more than I needed to – but you should know me by now.

Out of the reporters' group, only Spencer, Grisha, and I know what happened to Qo'ai-Marael. I can tell

Bluefeather and Khaldun are itching to ask, so I have to act before they do. Spencer gives me the nod. I explain that the elder is presently indisposed and that her status is to remain undetermined for the rest of the celebration. I don't mean to be dishonest, but I'm operating along guidelines. It was clear from the beginning that our individual reports would stay confidential until the time of publishing – the reason is to avoid bleed-overs for the sake of authenticity. Of course, Le Lien has a responsibility to inform the assembly of what has happened, but not until the gathering comes to an end. It all sits squarely within the criterion of disclosure. It's trickier when direct questions are asked – we do not lie but we give two options: abide to the code of confidentiality or rescind the query.

The job of chronicling for the History department was benign enough to allow for some fun time with my friends – instead it turned into a regular job. I'm not complaining – I got close to Enola and that was an education. The most intriguing part – I confess – was to work with Sam. What was that exactly?! A piece of me begs to let it go – to conclude he's just a blissed-out soul, oblivious to his own limitations – but isn't that the essence of the mystery?

It's fitting that I should be thinking about Sam just as he and Vac emerge from one of the cabana portals. The three of us take off for a walk along the creek, away from the action, to go over our achievements and failures in the tunnels.

"I think it's time for me to go," Sam says.

"Go where?" I ask.

"I like you a lot, Milady, but I have other businesses back home that call for my attention. It was nice meeting you. Goodbye, Sir Vac," he says

He goes towards the water and he's gone in a blink – just like that.

"That's Sam..." Vac let off.

"You mean to tell me that he returned to his world without the help of the stones?" I ask, in a daze.

"Home is where the heart is, love is the path. Beside that, I don't know how he does it. I'm not one to mess with a good secret. If I were you – I would leave it at that."

Oh, Sam, for a minute I thought you were just a dumb, lucky dog... the irony!

–Angel Vera–

48 – CLOSING REPORT FROM BLUEFEATHER

Place of activity: Great Goddess Ma-l's domain
Date: year 1 of the Ma-lean calendar, G-day 7
Chronicler: Angel Bluefeather
Department of Warrior and Realm History

Evening is slowly moving over the grand gathering. The performances are ending, while Angels are steadily returning to the Great Hall. The last night is reserved for the official invitees, the small group that was instrumental to the successful, fragile, final steps of the realization of the realms as an emerging Oneness. We, chroniclers are to partake as we compose our closing reports – though it seems most of us are finished with the task and are being seen reveling – quite deservingly so, I may add. Since I've been chosen to write a summary, I'll serve double duty by combining it with this final report.

I was stationed on the celebration grounds for the entire length of the gathering – and so was Angel Khaldun, I believe. I am aware much happened beyond these portals during that time – I don't mean that lightly. The absence of my beloved Vera, who was assigned to the job of chronicling from the bustle of the kitchen, was most perplexing – especially when it conveyed that sense of urgent secrecy. I may not be a master of nuance like my good friend Khaldun, but I doubt any attentive Angel wouldn't be aware of a drama unraveling in the background. Lillian and Liv were also alternatively absent – when Le Lien is restless, one should better believe there is a valid reason for it.

That being said, I don't see the need to speculate on the item any further. The gathering was a resounding success, and Ma-l appears much enlivened by it.

Many relationships were made over the week – most certainly as the result of the influence of the hostess's environment. It surprises me that elders such as Tealsky and Niamh didn't fall to the spell of love – it takes much shielding from its goodness to become that immune to it.

The general overview of the gathering could most assuredly fit into a single report – but the more the merrier. Though much joy was shared and many alliances were made, I am left with the underlying sense of something missing. Perhaps I expected more romanticism, more prominent love-making, more freedom of spirit. Somehow, there was a perplexing aura of shyness around it, a lack of exuberance, as if something was holding it off – a message that said, "We're not quite there yet." Of course – because of my work – I could be misled as to the true significance of the celebration, so love may not be all there is at its core. Though I have to say – generally speaking – no shadow hovers above love like it did here.

When Qo'ai-Marael proposed to document the gathering, I was driven to believe a single chronicler positioned in Ma-l's realm was going to suffice – I volunteered for the task. After she insisted on having reports taken from various vantage points, I became confused as to her intentions. Anyone could have made a passing mention of the heightened intensity in the Great Hall, and the thought of embedding Monique and Gretchen in Xarn and Enola's realms, still appears far-fetched to this day. Now, in the light of the Master's absence, I wonder if there wasn't greater purpose to that choice. What did she intend on achieving by having reporters strategically located? I know there is something I am touching on, yet uncertainty makes it difficult to delve on the motives. When all the accounts are put together, I am convinced it will all make sense. For now I have to trust that Qo'ai-Marael had ample reason to choose so many of us.

As expected, each of the chroniclers probably wrote enough to fill a volume of mostly repetitive events. The reason for the length of the gathering was that it would allow for every Angel to enjoy at least one day on the grounds without overcrowding the ceremony. I expect substantial editing. I was told in advance that my most sexually provocative work would end up being left out. I don't mind whatsoever, since it only takes very few words to get things going. After all, we do not need to pretend that a quality that is so inherently part of us while in the physical form, does not exist – it's positively vibrant and unavoidable. I figure that all of the non-Angels, and particularly the readers from the many variances of evolved Earth, will allow their imagination to take over. But I have said enough already.

I am meant to meet with the others at some point in the next few days for a broader recap. Eventually, we will all be immersed in the making of the final manuscript with our editor, Angel Tamas. No doubt that by the time of publishing, we will have reached consensus on its contents.

So here we are, sisters and brothers, Angels and Earth dwellers, lovers of all provenances; the party is ending with a few dear friends around the last of the bonfires. There is laughter coming from Lillian and Geir's corner. Vera is leaning against me, talking with Khaldun and Xarn. I hear lovely Liv, who finally has dropped the mask of seriousness, Monique, Gretchen, and Grisha opting for a dip in the creek. Olaf and Marshall reminisce about old memories of the world they once shared...

I could go on and on, but what's more to say when all is good in Ma-l's realm!

Much love to all!

–Angel Bluefeather–

49 – A NOTE FROM GREAT GODDESS MA-L

The history department asked if I would be willing to add a few words about my personal experience around the Grand Gathering, so here it is:

The honor that was bestowed upon me by the many who visited, will be cherished for the remaining of eternity. I was able to give back from the beds of my own gardens – and I mean that in more ways than one – to those who gifted me with the opportunity and the tools to become one of the many deities of the realms. I am forever at their service, in spite of their wish to serve my creation.

When Great One Amaterasu invited us to the top of her glass pyramid to meet the One, I wasn't sure what to expect. Although I am the One of my land, the collective reality of the realms adds up to a whole whose breadth may leave one yearning for comprehension – even with only the three of us so far. Now I understand what lies ahead.

But a Goddess of her land doesn't just busy herself with her own kitchen and gardens – she is her land. So when darkness hovers like in the days before the battles, she knows something is not quite right with her universe. Whatever it was that loomed over it, I am glad it's now fully gone. I saw it on Enola and Xarn's faces, especially Enola – she felt it like an arrow traveling towards her heart. There could have been more, but four came to the gathering – two pairs who watched as if to take a last look before it was all gone. Angel Bluefeather did his best to hand two of them a gift of love, but love was not what they came here for. Eventually, Vac – when he returns from

Amaterasu's domain – will no doubt explain what did happen. Overall, it leaves one to wonder about the forces that push against our emerging Oneness. Did we pose a direct threat, or were we caught in between factions battling each other? As much as I would wish otherwise, I sense this is not yet over with. The fact one hundred and twenty-nine realms have not responded to the call of the lanes is grounds for discomfort. Great One Amaterasu is quick to point that these worlds will open their gates when ready, but she also says that their lateness stifles the growth of the collective gestalt – so why muddy the narrative? I am quite certain something is amiss with them; so that's why Xarn, Enola, Saka, and I will dedicate much of our energy to come to the rescue of these domains and the realms as a whole.

I am aware I'm supposed to be writing about my impression of the gathering, but all is tied. This was a celebration of the rise of the realms away from the mother reality – there will be another about their convergence – this time, instead of a chronicle, it will be an entire chapter of history.

In perspective, the events that followed Olaf and Vac's entry into my pocket reality, felt like they covered more time than the millennia spent in the stone – their intensity made up for the difference. My world has become a much bigger place with Olaf and Saka in it, even if the Goddess of Light spends most of her time with Xarn. But wherever her destiny takes her, that light of hers will forever shine on my world as it does in my heart.

END NOTE

The Department of Warrior and Realm History is honored to introduce the Chronicle of Ma-l's Grand Gathering as the pivotal historical event that symbolically defines the emergence of the new Oneness. All of what was reported by the eight writers and left out of the publishing, has been archived and can be viewed upon signing as a guest. We regret that information will not be available to the reader from the sentient species without access to our network, unless of course, they ask an Angel – we are fairly certain one is readily available for support in their neighborhood or district.

We are quite aware that the whole of this short list of reports adds up to an intriguing story around the interference of XVII. Whether the placement of the chroniclers was orchestrated or resulted from harmonic spontaneity, it is not known. Needless to say, without that particular arrangement, you, the reader, wouldn't be in possession of this manuscript, or aware there was ever such a thing as the realms of the Warriors. Unfortunately, senior historian, Qo'ai-Marael, who would be the one to ask about it, is no longer with the department.

–Angel Tamas, editor–
Warrior and Realm History